Elisabeth

and the
Windmill

Books by Esther Bender

Lemon Tree Series
Katie and the Lemon Tree
Virginia and the Tiny One
Elisabeth and the Windmill

Picture Storybooks
April Bluebird
The Crooked Tree
Search for a Fawn

Mystery
Shadow at Sun Lake

Meditations
A Cry from the Clay

Elisabeth
and the
Windmill

Esther Bender

Herald
Press

Scottdale, Pennsylvania
Waterloo, Ontario

14135230

Library of Congress Cataloging-in-Publication Data
Bender, Esther, 1942-
  Elisabeth and the windmill / Esther Bender.
        p. cm. — (Lemon tree series ; 3)
Summary: Elisabeth, sixteen-year-old granddaughter of
German immigrants, is torn between two indentured ser-
vants from Germany, mischievous Hannes, who is teach-
ing her to read, and serious kind Milo.
  ISBN 0-8361-9204-4 (pbk. : alk. paper)
  [1. Frontier and pioneer life—Fiction. 2. German
Americans—Fiction.
3. Christian life—Fiction. 4. Family life—Fiction.
5. Reading—Fiction.] I. Title.
  PZ7.B43137El 2003
  [Fic]—dc21

                                        2002155322

Unless otherwise noted, Scripture is from the *King James Version.*

ELISABETH AND THE WINDMILL
Copyright © 2003 by Herald Press, Scottdale, Pa. 15683
    Published simultaneously in Canada by Herald Press,
    Waterloo, Ont. N2L 6H7. All rights reserved
Library of Congress Catalog Card Number: 2002155322
International Standard Book Number: 0-8361-9204-4
Printed in the United States of America
Design by Jim Butti / Sandra Johnson
Art by Joy Dunn Keenan

10 09 08 07 06 05 04 03 10 9 8 7 6 5 4 3 2 1

To order or request information, please call
1-800-759-4447 (individuals); 1-800-245-7894 (trade).
Website: www.mph.org

**To Dot, my sister,
who was the cartwheel girl.**

Contents

The Promises!
The Dreams!

Katie and the Lemon Tree tells how Katie Miller comes to America in the early 1800s with her young husband, Daniel. They land in Baltimore, buy a horse and wagon, and travel west into the mountains. There they buy inexpensive land and find settlers willing to help them build a cabin. Winter is coming.

When they unpack, Katie finds a lemon that she picked up on the dock when they landed in Baltimore. Rotten now, the lemon yields seeds which Katie plants in a cup. A few seeds sprout and grow. From these seeds, a lemon tree grows. But how can a lemon tree bear fruit in Maryland where winter blizzards blow? Katie calls on faith that can move mountains—that fulfills promises and dreams.

What promises? The promise that they wouldn't be hunted down in America for belonging to a church that baptizes adult believers. The promise that they can buy land and keep it for their children in America.

What dreams? The dream that all the members of their family can come to America, too. The dream of having enough money in America. The dream of praying any time they want without anyone hurting them.

A silent teacher, the lemon tree becomes a symbol of faith for Katie. Faith is in the struggle to water and care for the seed, even though many years pass before the tree bears fruit. Faith is what helps Katie believe the fruit will come.

Virginia and the Tiny One and *Elisabeth and the Windmill* are both stories about Katie and Daniel Miller's grandchildren. Virginia is the daughter of Daniel, Katie's oldest child. She is a year older than her cousin, Elisabeth. Elisabeth is the daughter of Dorcas, Katie's middle child.

In *Virginia and the Tiny One,* Virginia perseveres in the care of triplet babies in a time when baby bottles and disposable diapers are unknown. Virginia learns that promises must be kept, even to oneself. Miracles, although prayed for, may take a lot of hard work and faith.

Virginia has a dream for little Louis whom she calls Tiny. Tiny may be a doctor someday or perhaps the President. But it will take faith to even keep him alive. Virginia has one thing to look forward to—the spelling bee. Even that may be taken from her but perhaps not if she can study at home.

Now in *Elisabeth and the Windmill*, Elisabeth has a secret that haunts her: she cannot read.

She has had to stay home from school many days to help with her large family who live at Fog Hill. She has helped with maple sugaring in the spring and butchering in the fall. When she recited in first grade and the children laughed, she began to give up.

When Elisabeth's family moved to the second house in Grandma Katie's yard, Elisabeth was fourteen. Now sixteen, Elisabeth faces the truth. Her school days are over and she can't read. Papa says girls don't need to know how to read. But like her Grandma Katie, Elisabeth dreams too—she dreams of reading.

Elisabeth's emotions turn upside down like the windmill turning by the greenhouses when Hannes offers to teach her to read and she finds herself in a close situation with Milo, the indentured servant working for her Grandpa. There are two immigrant young men in her life. Will she love one of them? Which one?

Elisabeth likes to turn cartwheels. She likes to go barefoot. As the wind blows hither and yon, so are the winds of the spirit, sometimes turning her up! Sometimes down! Like the windmill she watches, it keeps turning and turning.

Listen! They are coming to America!
Hear them! Waves of immigrants from Germany!

What brings them to America?
Poor flax crop and potato blight.
Revolution and debtor's plight.
Soldiers who come for believers at night.
Young men taken and made to fight.
Fear to worship by light of day.
No more land to be sold away.

How, without money to buy their way?
The captain will let them sail without pay.
In America, the captain will be paid
By men who bid for the contract
Made for five years or ten—whatever agreed.

So come, people of Germany, sail on!
Welcome to America!

1

Elisabeth and the Windmill

Sixteen-year-old Elisabeth looked quickly around the yard on her way from the chicken house. Satisfied she was alone, she set down her egg basket. She took a quick running jump, landed on her hands, and cartwheeled down the lawn, going over so fast and straight that her skirts clung to her. The tall pine tree whirled upside down and righted itself four times.

Oh, I do love the feel of turning over! How would the world look if the clouds were under my feet and the green lawn hung upside down?

She pulled out hairpins that had loosened from her dark braids and poked them back in. Picking up her egg basket, she paused to enjoy the sunny day. This was her favorite time of year, the first of June.

She admired the two freshly painted white

houses, the smaller one the home of her Grandpa, Grandma, and Grandma's mother. Elisabeth's family lived in the larger house. They had moved there just two years ago when Aunt Maria and Uncle Louis moved out and built their own house a mile down the road. Elisabeth loved having Grandma Katie so close, but now she looked over her shoulder to see if Grandma was watching. She knew Grandma would scold gently if she saw her cartwheeling in the yard. But she saw no sign of her.

The yard was still wet with dew and a golden spider web swayed on a lilac in the sun. Elisabeth breathed deeply of the fresh scent. Her eyes traveled around the circular flower beds and borders that came from Grandma Katie's artistry. At one edge of the lawn, side by side, were three long greenhouses with gardens between them. The lawns and houses were surrounded by a white picket fence that ended at the greenhouses.

Above the greenhouses, a windmill turned lazily in the breeze, pumping water for the plants. Elisabeth heard its scree-ee-ch in her mind. Outside the yard fence was a small barn for the cows and horses, a building that housed pigs downstairs and chickens upstairs, an old log shed at the back of the garden, and a buggy shed.

Elisabeth's mind wandered to the young man who would be coming soon from Germany—an indentured servant, although her family never used that name. Grandpa and Grandma had invited Milo Schrag to come work in the green-houses after receiving a letter from his mother begging them to pay his ship's passage in return for five years of work. She was close to death and wanted to see him reach America before she died. Grandma and Grandpa had agreed and sent him a contract. Then they had received a letter from Milo saying his mother had died, but he wanted to come anyway. Grandpa Daniel sent money to Baltimore to pay his passage. He should be here any day now. She gazed at the greenhouses without seeing them, trying to guess how Milo might look. He was eighteen, Mama had said. He had dark hair and —

Suddenly, she heard a scuffling sound above her, then a chuckle. The chuckle was familiar. Her face flushed as she looked up. She saw only boots in the pine tree, but she knew that voice.

"Hannes Weaver!" she cried, remembering that she had cartwheeled below him. "How could you? How could you watch me?"

She heard him laugh, then heard the scratching of his boots. A pair of long legs appeared, followed by slim hips and broad shoulders, then a shock of golden hair above a sun-freckled mischievous face. His wide mouth was set in a big grin. Elisabeth thought he was old, possibly twenty-one or twenty-two. And he was a tease.

"Why, Lizzie! You went over so fast and straight, I didn't see more than the bottom of your skirts."

She looked at him in exasperation, her dark eyebrows knitting over her blue-gray eyes. "Hannes, you know better than to watch a lady do her daily drills," she said.

"I know better. I just couldn't help myself. I looked down to see where to put my foot and I saw you. Before I knew it, you were turning like that windmill. Do you think God will forgive me for watching you?" The mischief in his blue eyes confused her.

"Of course, God will forgive you, but. . . ." Her sentence remained unsaid.

She was thinking that she wasn't wearing shoes or stockings. She knew her mother would say, "Elisabeth, you know that a lady always wears stockings." And Mama always wore stockings.

But Grandma, well, she had excused herself by thinking that Grandma Katie didn't wear stockings in the garden. A chicken house was only a little less messy than a garden—or messier, depending how you thought about it.

Hannes took the basket of eggs from her hand. "Do you wash these at the pump before taking them to the house?" he asked, changing the subject.

"Yes, I do."

"Then let me wash them today to atone for my eyesight."

Elisabeth knew, without looking, that his blue eyes would be dancing. They walked toward the pump in the lawn under the pine trees. Hannes pumped water with one hand and washed the eggs, one by one, with the other. He handed the basket of clean dripping eggs to her.

She took the eggs from him and felt water drain from the eggs onto her feet. She wrinkled up her toes and wished she had her shoes and stockings on. She felt like a little girl in her bare feet.

"What are you doing here today?" she asked.

"Here?" he asked. "I came to see your father. He told me he has some soft wood for me to carve."

"Wood to carve? Why do you want to carve wood?"

"To make pictures for the paper," he replied.

"What paper?"

"It's called *The Windmill Turns*," he replied. "It's not Mr. Burger's regular paper. It's one I write about special things. Mr. Burger lets me plan it like I wish. Haven't you heard of it?"

She shook her head and said sadly, "I can't read very well."

"Why not?" he asked, surprised.

"Reading is hard for me. I don't understand how. I missed a lot of school because I had to help Mama with the babies. I just couldn't catch up. Papa says reading isn't so important for girls. They should be able to read and write their names and know the alphabet and a few words. I know some German words and how to spell our names. Papa says no more than that is necessary, but I want to read English."

17

Hannes's eyes had become thoughtful. He said, "Come visit the print shop. I'll teach you to read."

She glanced quickly at him to see if he was laughing. He wasn't. His eyes held a gentle good humor.

Elisabeth said, "I'll try to come but I can't promise. Sometimes we are very busy. A mile is a long way to walk for nothing."

"For nothing? Learning to read is nothing? I'd walk ten miles to learn to read."

Ten miles! How can learning to read be that important?

Elisabeth's father, Andrew, came out of the house. Hannes strode forward to shake her father's hand. Watching them together, Elisabeth realized that her father had respect for this young man who had come to America as a redemptioner. She had heard her father and Hannes talk about Mr. Burger going to Baltimore and bidding for him. Hannes had said the bidding made him feel like he was a slave. He had been very young then. But Hannes had impressed her grandparents and parents so much that they were willing to send for Milo. Hannes and her father had become good friends in spite of the difference in their ages.

She left the two men and walked into the cool basement with the basket of eggs. *Can I really learn to read well? How can reading be that important?*

Then she thought of Hannes's blue eyes and

her fingers trembled as she took the eggs from the basket. *I would like to please Hannes.* She felt like the windmill, turning . . . pausing . . . turning . . . upside down!

Hannes is handsome. Hannes's mouth is too big. Turning . . . turning . . . right side up!

Hannes would make a good husband. I couldn't stand it if Hannes laughed at me. Turning . . . turning . . . upside down!

But Papa would never let me marry Hannes. Hannes is not in our church. But I could let him teach me to read. Turning . . . turning . . . right side up!

When the eggs were sorted by size into baskets by size and set by the watering trough to cool, she pulled on the stockings she had left in the basement. She tugged on her shoes and went outside. A dark cloud was coming up in the west. The windmill was turning rapidly.

Elisabeth felt her stomach churning like the windmill.

2

Crying in the Attic

She rushed into the house and fled to the attic. It was the only place she was sure no one would come. For the first time in her life, she allowed herself to feel grief about not being able to read. Tears ran down her cheeks. She relived first grade in the little schoolhouse at Fog Hill and felt again the pain of loneliness.

Her mother was Dorcas, Grandma Katie's middle child. Dorcas had married Andrew Brenneman and gone to live with him at Fog Hill. Elisabeth was born and grew up there. Fog Hill was only ten miles from Grandpa's house, but the road was steep and rugged. The school at Fog Hill had only five students besides Elisabeth and her brother and sisters.

Elisabeth often stayed home from school to help with the younger children. She stayed home in the spring when she was needed to help with maple sugaring. She stayed in the fall to help with butchering. Thinking about it now, she felt sad about her reading.

She remembered the day in first grade she realized the other children all could read words she didn't know. She had been absent several days. When she returned to school, Mr. Beachy said that letters have sounds. What could Mr. Beachy mean?

The children laughed at her when she didn't know the sounds of the letters. Then the teacher laughed — not a mean laugh. He probably wasn't even laughing at her, she realized now. From that day onward, she became more and more flustered each time it was her turn to read. Then one day, she started telling herself, "Reading isn't important anyway — not for girls." And she quit trying, refusing to recite.

Two years ago, the Brenneman family moved home to the greenhouses where her grandparents lived. Elisabeth had been present when they signed the agreement. She became aware then that her mother and grandmother, unlike most women she knew, could sign their names and read a little. She was sure her mother could read some German, but she didn't know about English. Grandma Katie could read German. Could Grandma Katie read English? She wasn't sure, but she thought so. Elisabeth didn't understand why she, Elisabeth, couldn't read, too.

Suddenly, there in the attic, she found she was sobbing. Her handkerchief was soggy. She cried and cried without noticing the attic and its gloominess. The sounds of her sobs were drowned out by rain on the roof that added to her misery. Half an hour later, she blew her nose and pushed herself up from the wooden box she was sitting on. *Maybe I'll try again to learn to read. Maybe, maybe Hannes understands how and he can tell me. No, I don't want Hannes to teach me.* She had a mental image of the windmill turning. She was right side up one minute and upside down the next. She wanted to read. She didn't want to make the effort. She wanted Hannes to teach her. She didn't want Hannes to teach her.

She gradually became aware of the attic. Noticing the old camelback trunk, she opened the lid. Carefully she took out the items in the top. She knew what some of them were. Grandma Katie had told her. There was the old lantern Grandpa Daniel had brought from Germany. Here was the cook pot in which Grandma Katie had brought the lemon from Baltimore. And here was the cup in which she had planted the lemon seeds.

Elisabeth lifted yellowing linens from the chest. She knew Grandma had woven these fine linens from flax in Germany, before they came to America. And here was the enormous old German Bible, its pages falling out and the leather cover sprinkled with mildew. She opened it and fingered the pages carefully. Then she noticed the loose pages were upside down.

Carefully, she righted them. By looking closely at the numbers, she fit them in order. When she had finished, she gave a sigh of pleasure. She had accomplished an act of reading!

She felt hope. Then she lugged the huge book to the window and found the birth and death register. She could read it by thinking of the birth order of her brothers and sisters. They were all there: Elisabeth, Katerina, Jacob, Peter, Barbara, Maria, Adam, Leah, Anna.

A tiny ray of light began to shine. She, Elisabeth, would learn to read. Someday, some-how, she would learn to read. Even if she had to have Hannes teach her. A Bible verse, liberally interpreted in Grandma Katie's own words flashed through her mind: "If you wait for per-fect conditions, you will never get anything done." (Ecclesiastes 11:4)

In that moment, Elisabeth made a decision. She would learn to read and Hannes would teach her. And she would never let Hannes's teasing stop her.

3

Milo Arrives

In late afternoon of late June, Milo Schrag came walking from Shaw Mill. He had come by stagecoach, unannounced. Carrying a large case held together with rope, he stepped through the rose trellis at the edge of the lawn. Elisabeth stopped weeding flowers and stared. She knew him immediately from her mother's description.

He set the case down and looked at the lawn with its stately trees, shrubs, and flowers. He seemed to be in a daze. His clothes were threadbare and his hat squashed sideways. Elisabeth thought he must be surprised to find this garden spot at the end of a long dusty road. She left the pile of weeds and came to shake his hand. When she got nearer, she tried not to stare at a fresh scar above his eye. *What could have happened to him?*

"Welcome!" She held out a grubby hand, covered with rich soil. "You must be Milo Schrag."

He shook her hand. His fingers were strong, but his hands shook. Looking down, she saw that they were bony and calloused. His dark skin was tight and smooth across his cheekbones. He was a thin, wiry, young man who seemed ill at ease meeting her.

"I am here to work off my ship's passage. Mr. Miller paid my way," he said.

Elisabeth gave him a big smile and was glad she had even white teeth. "I am Elisabeth Brenneman, Mr. Miller's granddaughter," she said.

Her younger brothers, Jacob and Peter, were peeping from behind the cherry tree. She motioned for them to come. They came shyly up to find out who had come. "These are my brothers," Elisabeth told Milo. "Here, let me help you."

Quickly she picked up his case and began walking briskly down the walk to Grandma's house. Milo had no choice but to come running awkwardly after, followed by Jacob and Peter. By now, Barbara and Maria came running from the apple tree where they had been playing with their dolls. Elisabeth swung the kitchen door open. "Grandma," she cried. "Grandma!"

Katie Miller came from the parlor with some clothes she had been sewing draped over her arm. Her blue-gray eyes were shining. "Milo Schrag! You're here!"

She hugged the young man and said, "You

weren't born yet when I left Germany! And now your mother has died. I was so sorry to hear she had died."

"If only she could have come here with me. I didn't expect such a welcome!" Milo spoke softly and gently, tears in his eyes. His hands shook as before.

Maybe he is hungry.

She saw the quick tears in her grandmother's eyes. Grandma wiped her eyes on her apron. She covered her sadness by hustling around the kitchen, fixing a cup of steaming tea. She set it on the table and motioned for Milo to sit down. Milo seated himself and sipped the tea. Elisabeth thought his shaking hands looked sore and blistered and she could hardly keep her eyes off his scar.

Katie noticed, too, and said, "Milo, your hands! And your forehead! What happened?"

Milo looked at his hands and said, "I was assigned the ropes on the ship. They assigned jobs, the hardest jobs to the indentured servants. They knew we had no one to complain to. As for my forehead, we were barely gone from Germany when a storm at sea threw me across the deck and I struck my head."

"Well, I will be sure Daniel knows about your hands and lets you have a day or two to heal before you begin your work," said Katie. "I'm really sorry about your head, but I'm so glad you are safely here. We've been looking for you to come for some time now. Are you hungry?"

"I am hungry," he said. "I paid all my money for the coach, so I haven't eaten in two days."

"Goodness!" said Katie. "Run get some ham from the cellar, Elisabeth. We will fry some up good for a sandwich."

While the wonderful smell of smoked ham frying filled the kitchen, Elisabeth asked, "Did you have a good trip coming over on the ship?"

"We had several storms at sea. Everyone was sick and six died."

The house was so still the ticking clock in the next room seemed to echo in the kitchen. At last, Milo added, "Then when we were on the stagecoach, about fifteen miles east of here, we came through the shades, they call them. Dark pine forests. Two men robbed the stage. They took my watch, the one my father gave me." There was deep sadness in his voice. Even Katie was speechless when he told about the watch.

In spite of sadness, Elisabeth saw Milo's brown eyes gleam when he looked at the skillet in which the ham was sizzling and giving off a rich aroma. Grandma Katie's mother came in the kitchen. The elderly lady, nearly ninety years old, had lived many years in Germany. Now she said, "Who have we here? Let me guess. You are Elizabeth and Norman Schrag's grandson!" She clasped his hands in her pleasure, then continued chatting while busily making her own tea.

Elisabeth took the ham from the frying pan and put a thick slice in bread, added a few homemade sweet pickles and a hard-boiled egg, and handed Milo the plate. Milo stretched his tense fingers and put down his plate. He took a bite from the sandwich. It seemed to Elisabeth that he was trying not to gobble. She saw him relax his hand around the teacup. She gave her great-grandma a smile of gratitude. Great Gram's chatting was annoying sometimes, but it was also so free and easy that she made people feel at home.

Milo ate rapidly, then slowed down, taking smaller bites as though he suddenly remembered his manners. At last he nibbled the cookies Elisabeth brought with obvious pleasure and slowly sipped the tea. When he had finished everything, polishing his plate of the last crumbs, he said, "I have a gift for you." He unwrapped the rope from around his suitcase and reached inside. He took out a ceramic mug with a design on the side.

"It is the Mueller's family design. It was in my mother's possessions and I saved it for you," said Milo, handing the mug to Katie. Elisabeth knew that Grandpa Daniel's family name had been Mueller instead of Miller in Germany.

"Oh, thank you. I will show Daniel. He will be pleased," said Grandma Katie. She turned the mug slowly. Her eyes had a far-away dreaminess. Elisabeth knew she was thinking of the life she had lived before coming to America.

"Take Milo and show him to his room," said Grandma at last, looking at Elisabeth.

Milo followed her, carrying his stuffed case with the rope dragging on the floor. Elisabeth led the way up the stairs and around the turn to the back of the house. Barbara and Maria followed too.

"Here it is," said Elisabeth, throwing open the door of a small room below the eaves. "It's not very big," she apologized.

The room held a bed with a crazy patch quilt on top, a chest, a lantern hanging on a nail, and a small desk with a pen and a bottle of ink.

"This is large compared to room on board the ship. Oh, I see a pen and ink. I will write to my grandma this day," said Milo. "She will be glad to hear I arrived safely. We set sail nearly six weeks ago and I haven't had a chance to write to her yet."

For the first time in her life, Elisabeth wondered how it would feel to be a mother or grandmother staying behind in Germany. Would she worry about her son? Or would she come to America herself as Great Grams had done.

Milo and Hannes. Both young men had come to America from Germany. Both had signed papers to work for someone until their ships' passages were paid and they were free. She knew nothing of the life Hannes had lived, but she thought she knew much about Milo. Milo was from the same village as her grandmother, although he was born after she left. Milo—was he kin?—at least, he was a neighbor. He was already like family. Elisabeth knew there was no reason for the feeling she had about him. He was just familiar.

Angelface, her cat, rubbed against Milo's leg. He picked her up. "May I keep her up here with me awhile?" he asked. "She seems to like me." He stroked the whiskers on her white angel wings, the markings on her face for which she was named.

Elisabeth nodded. She went to stand by him at the window. The windmill was visible beyond the greenhouses, spinning briskly in the breeze. He said softly, "The same wind turns the windmills in Germany."

"Sometimes fast, sometimes slow, and sometimes not at all," said Elisabeth, startled at the comfortable feeling that accompanied her own words.

"And today, I am grateful to be here . . . and the wind blowing. . . ." Milo's voice trailed off.

Elisabeth called to her little sisters and they backed out the door. Milo shut it softly.

Barbara and Maria giggled. On the way downstairs, Barbara said, "Of course, the wind blows in Germany. He's funny, but I like him. Do you think he will be like our big brother after awhile?"

Maria said scornfully, "He's too old for that, Barbara."

"He is not! If he would marry Elisabeth, he would be our brother."

Elisabeth felt her face flush. "Now, girls! He's not going to marry me."

"Why not?" asked Barbara and Maria together.

"Oh, because—" said Elisabeth. Still, she had a mental picture of her and Milo walking hand in hand.

4

With Milo to the Village

Elisabeth lay in bed, eyes still shut, letting the first rays of the sun turn the bedroom into a golden, warm palace. In this dreamy state, her mind roved freely, turning up images like fish worms in fertile greenhouse soil. Suddenly, an image of boots in the top of a tree brought her sharply alert. *What had Hannes been doing in the top of the tree anyway?*

She didn't move a muscle, just lay wondering. She could think of no reason. She would ask him next time she saw him. When would she see him? Already several weeks had passed and she had made no attempt to go to the print shop. *Today, I will see Hannes. I will go to the print shop.* She sprang out of bed.

But Papa had other plans for her. "I must see that Milo has new boots. His boots have holes in them from walking so far. And I am too busy in the fields to take him. Elisabeth, I want you to go with Milo to the village and buy boots for him. Your Mama will need some things from the store, too."

Elisabeth and Milo did as Papa said. Milo packed the eggs under the seat of the small buggy, then hurried to give Elisabeth a hand before swinging into the driver's seat himself. The old horse, Jingles, was the only one Papa could spare from the fieldwork. Milo kept a firm grasp on the reins but Jingles could have found the way alone.

"Back to Shaw Mill," said Milo. "I don't think I really saw it when I came. I was too worried about meeting your family."

Elisabeth was glad to tell Milo about her family. "You probably didn't meet them all yet. There's Katerina. She's fourteen. Then Jacob and Peter. They're thirteen and twelve. Barbara's nine and Maria's eight. Adam's five, Leah's four, and Anna's a baby. My papa's mother was Irish, so that's where Papa gets his reddish curly hair. I get curly hair from Papa and dark hair from Mama, but Katerina's hair is reddish and curly. So is Maria's and Adam's." Elisabeth chattered on and on and Milo listened attentively.

When they came to the print shop, Elisabeth pointed it out to Milo. "Hannes lives there. He likes to tease and sometimes I get so upset at him when he won't be serious. Hannes said he'd teach me to read English. I don't know if Papa will let me learn or not. If I were learning

German, Papa would say I could use what I'd learned to read the Bible. But we don't read English in church."

"Reading English is important," Milo said gravely.

"Why?" asked Elisabeth.

"I'd like to read English too. My papers for the ship's passage are written in English. If your grandfather weren't an honorable man, he could cheat me. There are English-speaking people all around us. It's good to read German, but it's good to read English, too. Yes, it's really important to read English." Milo spoke earnestly.

They had come to the village. Elisabeth went with Milo into the store. Milo tried on a pair of boots and said they were fine, but Elisabeth was afraid they had cardboard soles and insisted on a pair with good leather soles. Milo agreed only after blushing with embarrassment. "A woman shouldn't—you shouldn't have to pay for—Mr. Miller has done enough for me," he said.

On the way home, Milo began to talk about the voyage to America.

"How much does it cost to come to America?" asked Elisabeth.

"It cost me 220 dollars," he said. "Others who were paying in German money had to pay thirty German talers."

Elisabeth giggled. "Talers! Papa says that the English word dollars comes from the German talers. I think that's funny. The English use the German."

"Dollars or talers, I don't know whether 220 dollars or 30 talers is more."

"I don't know which is more either. Were there children on the ship?" asked Elisabeth.

"Yes, and parents didn't have to pay for the young children. There were nearly thirty of them."

"Where did you sail from?" asked Elisabeth.

"From Bremerhaven near the mouth of the Weser River. The papers say Bremen to Baltimore, but we had to go to Bremerhaven to get on the ship."

"Why did your mother want you to come to America?" asked Elisabeth.

"We had potato blight for several years in a row. And the other crops did poorly. We couldn't buy any more land because the government wouldn't let us. And we were weaving linen from flax for part of our money and the flax crop was poor. But I tell you, the worst is worshiping in secret. We were afraid to worship as we wanted. We—the people in my community—feel sure there will be a revolution soon any day now. The government is taking the younger men to fight wars. We lived in fear every day. I still get awake at night, sweated, and afraid that soldiers are coming to get me."

Milo shivered. Elisabeth had a flash of fear for him, but knowing he was safe, it faded quickly.

They had reached the lane to the greenhouses. Milo slowed the horse and let him plod to the buggy shed.

"Whoa, whoa!" Milo's voice was steady. He backed the buggy into the shed. Elisabeth admired the way he methodically wrapped the reins so they wouldn't tangle.

As they went in the walk together, Milo said shyly, "I'm really glad I'm here in America. Are you . . .? How old . . .?" He fell silent. His new boots echoed on the flat stone in the yard.

Elisabeth didn't know what he intended to say, but she suspected he was going to ask her age. Why would he ask her age? She told her heart to stop pounding.

At Grandma's house, Elisabeth went inside with Milo to talk to Grandma. Milo went upstairs immediately. Grandma asked what Milo talked about on the way to the village. Elisabeth said she had told Milo about her family and Milo had told about Germany and the voyage over.

"Milo pleases me well," said Grandma Katie. "I think we made a good decision to bring him to America."

When Elisabeth went back to her own house, she looked back at Grandma's house. She felt a pang of jealousy when she saw Angelface pacing back and forth in Milo's open bedroom window. Milo had made a friend of her cat and probably didn't even know it was hers.

What if Milo had been going to ask her age? Was he wondering if she was old enough to be interested in him? If she was old enough to marry? Marrying Milo would make Grandma

36

Katie happy. Grandma had said, "Milo pleases me well."

Elisabeth sighed. She would like to please Grandma, too. She turned and looked back at the window once more. Now Milo was there holding Angelface. He waved and she waved back. She swung open the summer door and went inside.

5

The Windmill Turns

July began with a heat wave that left everyone feeling drained. "I feel as lazy as that windmill," said Mama to Elisabeth as they washed the breakfast dishes. Elisabeth paused to watch the windmill.

"The windmill does cartwheels!" said Elisabeth. *But which is the upside down?* The windmill reminded her of Hannes and the reading lesson she had been promised. She still hadn't gone to see him. She would do something about it this very day.

When the dishes were done, Elisabeth said to Mama, "Maybe I could go to the store after the greenhouse work is done and get those things you mentioned the other day."

"I want to go with her," said Katerina. "Please."

"I want to go by myself, Katerina. I'll wash all the supper dishes by myself if I can go alone," Elisabeth begged.

"I'm surprised, Elisabeth. You don't want company on the way? You went last week and didn't remember all my things. Katerina could help you remember," said her mother. Then she gave in, "It will be hot today. I guess if you went alone you could take Fanny."

Fanny was the little mare Grandpa had bought for the women to ride. Elisabeth thought Fanny was tame and sleepy. She would rather have taken Jingles, although Jingles was so old he wore out quickly.

She said, "I'd like to walk. If I hurry, could I stop at Mary's house and see her?"

"You want to walk in this heat? Ach! Just be home by suppertime," said Mama. "We have greenhouse plants to water tonight."

Elisabeth hummed as she washed the noon dishes. Then she put on her sunbonnet to keep the sun from her face in the greenhouse as she set out two flats of lettuce. Two flats! That was what they set out nearly every day to keep the crop of lettuce maturing at an even rate. It was late for lettuce and nearly too hot. But the lettuce would mature in the "underground" greenhouse. It was the last greenhouse they had built, below ground level at one end to take advantage of the cooling of the earth.

Louis came whistling into the greenhouse. "Nearly finished already!" he exclaimed, observing Elisabeth's flying fingers. Uncle Louis was their salesman. Every day he packed the wagon and delivered fresh lettuce to the village.

The lettuce finished, she went to the yard pump to wash her hands. She stood thoughtfully under the pine tree. What was Hannes doing in that tree?

A sudden impulse overtook her. She swung lightly into the tree. She hadn't climbed this tree for a long time, but the branches were even and close. Staying close to the trunk, she went up the tree as easily as if it had been a ladder. At last, she was near enough to the top that the tree swayed with every step. She turned around, took a good grip on the tree—*ugh, sticky pine pitch*—and gazed over the countryside. She saw a panorama of the whole farm, the three greenhouses lined up like pea pods side by side, the windmill, the houses, the barn, the sheds, the chicken house and hog pen, the fruit orchard, the fence that went around the yard to keep out the cattle.

For the first time in her life, Elisabeth thought about all her family had. *We're almost rich. We have all these buildings and animals and beautiful lawns.* She looked beyond the yard to the fields. *There! A deer is eating with the cattle. We should name our farm—call it Deer Park Farm.*

She climbed down the tree hastily. As she walked to the house she wondered how to write *Deer Park.* She would make a sign for the farm. Now she suddenly had a burning reason to learn to read. She wanted to write *Deer Park.*

She set out quickly for the village with

Mama's list and the money tucked safely into her pocket. As soon as she was out of sight of the house, she began to jog at a steady pace. When she neared the print shop, she slowed to a decorous walk. Past the print shop and round the next turn, she began to jog again. In a few more minutes, she was in the village.

It didn't take long to purchase Mama's things. She made a quick trip down the street to Mary's house, chatted quickly over the fence with her, and headed for the print shop.

As she neared the shop, she felt her heart pounding harder than her rapid pace had caused. She wondered what the sign said over the print shop door. She stood, hesitantly touching the latch before she had the courage to squeeze it in her fingers and push the door open.

"Ah, ha!" Hannes boomed out. The door was barely open. "I'd begun to think you weren't coming. But it's good to see you. Come in, take off your bonnet, and watch what I'm doing." Elisabeth wondered how he could be so sure what she had come for.

On the table lay a large stack of papers. Elisabeth thought they probably were called *The Windmill Turns*. They were neatly printed in type Elisabeth could not read. She took off her bonnet and sat down on a stool in front of the table.

"Here, I'll show you how to do these. Then you can print while I rest."

Hannes rubbed paint over a woodcarving

done in the soft wood—yes, probably the soft wood he got from Papa.

He held the paper upside down over the woodcutting. Carefully, he lowered the paper onto the woodcut and rubbed it gently. When pulled away, his page was illustrated with—yes, she could hardly believe it, but it was an over-head view of the greenhouses—Papa's green-houses—as though a picture had been taken from the top of the tree! So that's what Hannes was doing in the tree! She felt relieved to think she knew the reason.

Hannes said, "The front page story is about your Papa, and how he and your Mama came to America, and how the people of Shaw Mill are grateful for the peace and prosperity they have found."

"I wish I could read it," she said.

"You will someday," Hannes said with confidence.

"How did you make the picture?"

"I used the soft wood your father gave me. First I drew it on the wood. Then I cut away the wood in the background. Then I inked the picture. The ink stayed on the high spots, so the paper printed only the high places on the paper."

Hannes let her rub the wood with ink and print the next paper. While she printed it, Hannes explained, "Woodcuts are an old way to make pictures. The only cost is a piece of wood to carve and some ink. I'm a bit of an artist, so I like doing them this way. Woodcuts were invented by the Japanese in the 1600s. This picture is only black and white, but if I had colored ink, I could make colored pictures."

Elisabeth inked and printed the fourth sheet as he told her about woodcuts. When he was finished, she said, "I think I had better go now. It's getting late."

That evening, Elisabeth told Milo and Katerina, "Hannes made a picture of our farm with a piece of wood and a knife. See!" She held up the paper and explained about the woodcut.

"I think I could make one. Follow me." Milo grinned.

"We don't have any wood," protested Elisabeth.

Milo took a knife from his pocket. He led the way through the barnyard into the woods. Carefully, he cut a design into the smooth wood of a tree. Then taking some pokeberries, he crushed some into the design. Katerina watched intently and exclaimed with surprise and delight as Milo took off his shoe and pressed the leather sole against the tree. The woodcut design came off on the sole.

"Milo, I do think you are the most inventive person I've ever known. Imagine, making a woodcut from a tree in the forest—on your shoe!" Katerina admired Milo's ingenuity.

Milo laughed. Elisabeth looked at him in surprise, thinking this was the first time she had truly heard him laugh. Milo laughing? How good that sounded!

Milo talked and laughed all the way to the house. He carried his shoe to show Grandma Katie. He told her, "I'll leave off my shoe at the door, then tomorrow I'll wear it outside until the picture wears off."

"Oh, Grandma Katie," said Katerina. "Isn't Milo smart!"

Grandma Katie said, "He certainly is!"

6

The Reading Lesson

A week later, Elisabeth sat at the table in the print shop. "Last week, we only had time to fold papers before you had to go home. Now let's see that you get a reading lesson," said Hannes.

He took one of the printed sheets from the scrap pile, looked at it for a moment, then selected a strip of type and cut it out. He handed it to her, saying, "This says, 'Daniel Miller raises lettuce in his greenhouse.' Now you repeat it to me."

Elisabeth repeated it, then her face felt hot. Her heart beat fast as the question she was burning to ask struggled inside her.

"I know 'Daniel Miller.' But how can you tell which other word is which?"

She had to know. After all, Papa might not let her come again. Today, she had been lucky enough to be sent to the store with a letter to Germany, but she must hurry again.

"You learn the rules of reading. All reading goes this way, left to right." He ran his finger under the line of type. "Then you say one word for each group of letters and you know which is which. After a while, you can read them mixed up, any way you want. But of course, you have to memorize the sentence exactly first. Won't work if you don't."

"I thought reading was something special. That's just plain—plain—work!" sighed Elisabeth.

"It's hard work at first, but the fun soon begins."

Elisabeth looked up into Hannes' face and his smiling blue eyes made her heart skip a beat. She had to pull her senses together to remember the question she was going to ask. At last she asked, "What fun?"

"I'm not telling," he said. "It's better if you discover it on your own. Now, do you have a pencil and paper?"

"Not of my own," she confessed. She felt angry. Why did he always confuse her? The windmill was upside down again.

She watched as he picked several sheets of smudged paper from a pile on the corner of the table. He pulled out a drawer and found several stubby pencils, sharpened them with a knife, and gave them to her.

"There you are! Writing is the upside down of reading so you should learn that too. Just copy the way the letters look. That will do for now. Next time you come to see me, bring those sheets filled up with 'Daniel Miller raises lettuce in his green-house.' Then you'll be well on your way to learning to read. That's the end of the lesson for today. Here's a free paper for your father. Sorry, it's a week late. Now you have to earn your lesson. Can you fold this stack of papers?"

"Sure, but you didn't say I had to pay for it!" she exclaimed as she began folding.

"A-ha, I like that! You're outspoken and want the truth!" he said.

His mouth is way too wide. She put that thought out of her head. She shouldn't think such things about her teacher.

He hummed as they both worked. In half an hour the whole stack was folded.

"Now you can tell your father you are working for me in exchange for learning to read. That makes my intentions good, doesn't it."

"Oh, yes. How did you think of that?" *Maybe his mouth isn't so wide, after all!*

She skipped down the road with a smile on her face. Now she could tell the truth in a way Papa would accept. *Thank you, God, for making it acceptable for me to read. Thank you that you are going to teach me. Thank you for Hannes. Thank you that he knows how to read. And I'm sorry I thought his mouth was too big. Amen.*

Suddenly she remembered. *Deer Park!* She had forgotten to ask how to spell Deer Park. Next time, she would remember.

She slowed to a walk and gradually became aware of the world around her. Clumps of green

47

unripe elderberries weighed down the bushes along the road, reminding her that they were excellent cover for bears. There weren't many bears around, but occasionally in berry season one wandered into farmland and caused a stir before going off to the miles and miles of forest that covered the ridges.

Raspberries thrust their long canes through the elderberries, providing fresh samples of the succulent fruit, but Elisabeth ignored them. She didn't want to meet any bears, so she began singing, forcing cheerfulness, letting them know by the sound of her voice that she was coming.

Elisabeth sighed with relief when she reached their own land. Here the cows had nibbled the grass and bushes down to short size. She could see the whole pasture of the farm she had begun to call Deer Park Farm.

What could I use to paint "Deer Park Farm"? At home, she searched the attic, the cellar, and the top of the barn to find a piece of board to paint the background. She would paint it white and have it ready to paint the letters by her next lesson. But try as she might, she could not find anything to paint.

That evening she asked Papa, "Do we have something to make a sign."

"No, we don't," said Papa.

Elisabeth sighed. She would have to tell Papa. Then the sign would have to wait until Papa was ready.

7

The Upside Down of Reading

At six o'clock in the morning, Elisabeth was already at work doing the laundry. Her groggy mind was stuck in a half-real, half-dream world. *Hannes Weaver! Hannes, a redemptioner. Martin Burger gone to meet the ship in Baltimore, bid on Hannes's ship passage, paid his way to come to America. Rub, rub, rub the clothes. Hannes working for Martin to pay back his ship fare. How long has it been since Hannes Weaver arrived? I lived at Fog Hill then. This soap is too oily. I didn't know Hannes then. I don't know how long ago Hannes came here.*

At six o'clock she just couldn't think clearly.

"Elisabeth!"

Elisabeth jumped and dropped the shirt she was washing on the washboard. "Oh, Grandma! You scared me!"

Grandma Katie churned butter in their cellar each morning. Now she looked at Elisabeth with a smile breaking up the wrinkles around her eyes. "You were dreaming. I think you were dreaming about Hannes Weaver. Dorcas—your Mama—doesn't notice because she's too busy, but I have time to notice the pink that touches your cheeks every time Hannes is mentioned. Am I right?"

"I think about Hannes," admitted Elisabeth, "but then I think I shouldn't think about Hannes because Papa would not want me to think about him. Sometimes I just think his mouth is too wide and he teases too much. But Grandma, I can't quit thinking."

"Hannes is a very handsome man," said Grandma. "I can't blame you for letting him take your heart. And I wouldn't be so sure about your Papa. He and Hannes have talked and. . . . you know that your secret is safe with me. Hannes has a generous mouth, but not too wide. Enough of Hannes. I think I know someone else who likes you. Milo is nearly your age, you know."

"Oh, Grandma, Milo is two years older. I'm not in love with Milo or anybody!"

Grandma's eyes crinkled again. "If you say all the potatoes are good, there's bound to be a rotten one in the bag."

"How do you think of all those things you say?"

"Easy," said Grandma. "Your great-great-grandma's words are in my head. When I hear my head say them, they pop out of my mouth."

"I guess the words people say make dead people seem alive," said Elisabeth. "I never knew great-great-grandma, but I know lots of things she said because you say them too."

"That's remembering. Writing is remembering on paper. It makes dead people seem alive!" said Grandma. "I wish your great-great-grandma had written down her sayings."

"You could write down the ones you can remember, couldn't you?" asked Elisabeth.

"Ach, yes, but it's too much trouble. I can't spell good."

"Grandma, why do you know how to read better than I do?"

"My father taught me in Germany. I guess here in America there is so much work to be done that learning gets neglected. Your mother never learned to read as well as I wished. And I can't read much English. Only German."

Elisabeth's hands began to move faster. She turned her attention back to the washing. Papa had such a large grass stain on his shirt. How would she ever get it out? She took the bar of homemade soap and rubbed the stain again. The oil in the soap began to dissolve the stain.

Hannes Weaver! Why can't I forget him? Ach! He means nothing to me.

At eight o'clock, Elisabeth was still washing clothes. Rubbing clothes on a hand board took a long time. Her back ached from bending over.

51

Mama came into the basement. Elisabeth said in a discouraged voice, "I don't think I'll ever get the clothes finished today."

Mama said, "I often think clothes are like the widow's oil and meal. The widow fed the prophet the last of her oil and meal, but when she went back, more oil and meal were in the cupboard. She made enough cakes to feed herself, her son, and the prophet. Every day after that, there was enough oil and meal for all of them. The clothes are the same. They are never all washed."

At last, the rag rugs were washed. They were saved for last because they were most grubby of all, covered with the dirt of shoes from three weeks of walking in the house. Elisabeth hung them on the clothesline.

She emptied the wash buckets and put away the washboard. Now she had a bit of free time. She would use it to study. She took the paper Hannes had given her to the front porch swing and wrote the assigned sentence without looking at the paper.

A shadow fell across her lap. She looked up. Milo!

"Where's Mrs. Miller?" he asked. "I've finished in the greenhouse and I want to know what to do next."

Just then Grandma Katie came out on the porch. She handed Elisabeth and Milo each a glass of lemonade, then sat down on the swing with Elisabeth. She motioned for Milo to sit in a porch chair. He barely sat down before

Angelface jumped on his lap. He stroked her fur and she settled down with a satisfied purr.

"You don't have to work every second," said Grandma Katie to Milo. "Sit and enjoy the day a little. You will find that at our house we don't expect more of you than we do of ourselves. We work hard, but we play too. Why come to America if we make slaves of ourselves to work?"

Milo had a dazed look on his face. He said, "Thank you, Mrs. Miller. I never hoped to find someone as kind as you."

Elisabeth's eyes met his for a little. He smiled, a shy smile. Elisabeth dropped her eyes to Angelface and said, "Angelface is my cat, but I think she loves you."

"Oh, my!" said Milo. "I didn't know Angelface was your cat. I wouldn't have tried to make such a pet of her." He sat there, looking uncomfortable.

Elisabeth felt her irritation toward Milo melt away. He was so obviously upset about having taken her cat as his own. She couldn't be angry at him. In fact, a tender feeling for him entered her heart. Looking in his dark eyes with their long lashes, she was glad that Angelface liked him.

8

Practicing and Singing

Elisabeth took the paper with her assigned sentence written on it, sped upstairs to her room, and quickly got out paper to check herself. Yes, she was right! To herself she whispered the words as she wrote them again, "Daniel Miller raises lettuce in his greenhouse." She had practiced all week to be ready for her next opportunity to see Hannes.

Now she suddenly turned the paper over and wrote, "greenhouse lettuce raises in Daniel Miller." She giggled. Yes, she knew the words well enough to turn them inside out! Now, for another lesson.

All day she thought about how she would see Hannes. *I could sneak over to the print shop. But then Papa would surely find out. Or I could tell Papa. That would be the honest way. But I am afraid. Oh, well, honesty is always the best, they say.*

At last, toward evening, she found her father in the barn. He was repairing the buggy.

"Papa," she said, "I know how to spell 'greenhouse.'"

"You do?" His voice showed surprise.

"G-R-E-E-N-H-O-U-S-E."

"How did you learn to spell that?"

"From Hannes Weaver."

A frown came over her father's face. "From Hannes?" His voice was questioning.

Elisabeth looked into her father's face. She could see that her father was feeling something he didn't like to feel. His eyes had a far-off expression. His lips were drawn into a thin line. Slowly, she began to realize something. *Papa can't read English either. He can read and write German because he learned it as a boy. But English! He knows no more English than I.*

At last, Papa said slowly, "You find learning to read English easy? You can do that?"

"Yes, Papa," she said. "The day Hannes came to see you, he said he could teach me to read. When I went to the village last Tuesday I folded newspapers for Hannes in exchange for a lesson. Papa, may I go work for Hannes again? I want to learn to spell *Deer Park Farm.* I want to make a sign for our farm."

Papa pulled his beard and rubbed his head as he always did when confronted by a perplexing problem. At last, he said, "I am going by the print shop tomorrow on my way to Shaw Mill. I will take you myself. Then there will be no questions from the neighbors."

"Oh, Papa! Thank you!" she exclaimed.

"I don't know if I am making a big mistake or not. If only you were a boy. Boys should learn to read and write English. But girls! Girls should learn the home skills." Papa was muttering to himself.

"But, Papa, America is different from when you first came here. Look at Auntie Barbara. Auntie Barbara runs a sawmill."

"Just because her husband is dead," said Papa.

"My husband may die," replied Elisabeth. "Or I may decide not to marry."

Papa resumed his work on the buggy. Elisabeth stood watching him. He looked up then and said, "Elisabeth, all I will promise is that I will let you learn *Deer Park Farm.* After that, I can't promise."

The next day dawned clear and sunny. Elisabeth was up with the birds to be sure she had all her work done before Papa left. When she climbed onto the seat beside Papa, she was singing softly under her breath. Like Grandma Katie, Elisabeth loved to sing.

Papa clucked to the horses. They were off to Shaw Mill. Elisabeth continued to sing.

"I still like the song about America," said Elisabeth.

"So do I," said Papa.

"Sing it, Papa," pleaded Elisabeth.

Papa cleared his throat. Then in rich, full tones he sang:

Und wenn wir sind in Balkmor,
Dann heban wir die Händ empor,
Und rufen laut Viktoria,
Jetzt sind wir in Amerika!

It was the "Good-bye Song" Grandma and Grandpa had sung when they left Germany. Elisabeth, listening to him, felt as though she knew Germany, as though she had left Germany, and as though Germany was her home, even though she had been born in America. She joined Papa in singing the verse in English:

When we come to Baltimore,
We'll hold our hands upraised,
And shout a word of victory,
Now we're in America!

The song rang through the forest. *If I could read English, I could read all of that song. It would be my song!*

At the print shop, Papa stopped the wagon and went inside with Elisabeth. Hannes was there working, but so was Mr. Burger.

"Come in, come in!" said Mr. Burger. "So, Elisabeth, you are an excellent paper folder. Hannes told me."

Elisabeth blushed. "I'm fast and I try to do it neatly." She felt even more flustered when Hannes winked at her.

Mr. Burger continued, "Hannes here, told me about you. Indeed, we do need someone to fold papers and clean up around here. Would you like to try the job? The paper comes out every Friday, so we need someone on Thursday morning for folding and afternoon for clean up. Wouldn't be a whole day, though."

"I will have to talk it over with Mama—and Papa," said Elisabeth, giving her father a smile. "But I would like to work today without pay while Papa goes to Shaw Mill. May I?" Elisabeth felt herself blushing again as she saw surprise in Mr. Burger's face.

"Hannes, how did you get this young lady to work for us without pay?" asked Mr. Burger.

"I didn't! I paid her," said Hannes. "I gave her a reading lesson."

"And I can spell every word you gave me," said Elisabeth.

"Folding the paper is worth more than that to me. I will pay you if you work today. Then I can work on my accounts in the back room. Hannes may give you a reading lesson, too, if he doesn't take too much time from work," said Mr. Burger.

Elisabeth looked at her father, seeing by the look on his face that he was uncertain about what to say.

"Oh, Papa, let me try it. I want to earn a little money of my own. You know how I have wanted a new bonnet. I could pay for it myself and save you the money," cried Elisabeth.

"As long as you will be here. . . ." said Papa, looking at Mr. Burger, hesitantly.

"I'll be here." Mr. Burger said firmly.

"Then I'll just be going on to town," said Papa. He turned and went out the door.

The minute Papa left, Mr. Burger disappeared into the back office.

9

Distractions!

Hannes was laughing with his eyes as he whispered loudly, "Mr. Burger hates to fold papers. He dislikes printing them even more. I knew I could get you a job because he doesn't have to pay you as much as a man." He was turning the hand press as he spoke. It spit out papers on a pile.

Hannes stopped printing and took papers from the bottom of the stack for her to fold. "The ink isn't dry enough on top. It would smudge and give you black hands."

When Elisabeth had settled into a routine, he demanded, "Spell 'greenhouse.' "

Elisabeth spelled each word for him as they folded. Then she said, "May I tell you the sentence to learn next?"

"Sure."

"Then how about: 'The deer eat grass at Deer Park Farm'?"

"Where is Deer Park Farm?" asked Hannes.

"Nowhere yet. But I like the name and deer do eat grass with our cows. I want to name our farm Deer Park Farm and paint a sign for it."

Hannes said, "I like your sentence, but I will change it just a little. It's always good to use some words you've learned so you don't forget them. How about: 'Deer eat the lettuce we raise at Deer Park Farm.' "

"But that's not true. The lettuce is in the greenhouse," she protested.

He grinned. "Use your imagination. Not every sentence must be true."

Elisabeth was surprised and disappointed. She had always been taught to tell the truth. Now she asked, "Do you write the truth in *The Windmill Turns?*"

"We try to write the truth, but what we are told is not always the truth or we use a word the people don't understand. Do you know what Thomas Jefferson said about newspapers?"

"What did he say?"

"He said the man who doesn't read anything is better educated than the man who reads *only* newspapers," quoted Hannes.

"How do you know—oooooh!" Elisabeth jumped up with a squeal. "Ooooooh!" She danced up and down, shaking her skirts.

Suddenly Hannes cried, "There it goes!" He grabbed the broom and began chasing a mouse around the room. Elisabeth grabbed her skirts tightly and stood on her chair. Mr. Burger, who had come from the other room, joined in the chase. At last puffing and red-faced, Mr. Burger said, "I give up. It's just a mouse." He disappeared into the back room.

"Elisabeth, you're having trouble with your skirts again!" exclaimed Hannes.

Elisabeth, who was getting down from the chair, slapped her hand on the table. "And you, Hannes, are too—too—you laugh at everything! I do believe you'd laugh at the Lord!"

"Yes, I would! The Bible says, 'Make a joyful noise unto the Lord.' Tell me how do you make a joyful noise without laughing?"

Elisabeth just looked at him. Frustration was in her eyes. She thrust out a dainty chin defiantly. "Hannes," she said, "Don't make fun of Scripture."

"I won't!" he replied.

His sober face satisfied her. She sat back with a big sigh. Then turning her attention back to the lesson, she said, "I know what we can use for a sentence. How about: 'The deer eat grass at Deer Park Farm and we eat the lettuce we raise at Deer Park Farm' "

"How will you remember all that?" asked Hannes.

"I made it up so, of course, I'll remember."

"You may change it this time. I'll write it for you." He took out pen and paper and began carefully writing out her sentence.

At that moment, the door burst open. A small boy pelted them with words in German.

Elisabeth understood his speech immediately.

She translated, "The store is on fire!"

Hannes burst out the door, ran to the shed and got a bucket, and headed toward the village. Elisabeth heard the small boy repeat his message inside the office as she ran after Hannes toward the village. She choked on the dust her long skirts stirred up on the road as she ran. As she topped the hill, a plume of black smoke rose from the store. *The post office is in the store! Our mail will be burnt up. What if Grandma got a letter from Germany! We may never see it. I couldn't read it anyway, but Grandma Katie could. Oh, I wish I could read like Grandma. I can't read English or German. Mama and Grandma don't even know how hard reading is for me.*

She stood in the crowd watching the fire. Suddenly, she heard footsteps and someone breathing hard behind her. She turned around. Milo! What was he doing here?

"Milo, how did you get here?" she asked.

"I ran from home," he said. "We weren't busy and Mr. Miller said I could come see what was on fire. We smelled smoke. I ran and now I'm going to help fight the fire as soon as I get my breath. I'm ready. I'll see you at home later."

Elisabeth watched Milo elbow his way through the crowd. He joined one of the chains of men who were passing buckets of water toward the fire. His thin wiry body moved in effortless rhythm, swinging the buckets.

Elisabeth could not help but admire the whole-hearted way he put himself into the job at hand.

Her eyes left Milo's back and, scanning the fire fighters, she saw Hannes. He too, was swinging buckets. As she watched, he climbed a ladder onto the roof and the chain moved up behind him, some men climbing onto the ladder handing buckets of water up to him. She shut her eyes so she wouldn't see the roof crumbling in, but when she opened them, the fire was nearly out. She stayed and watched until the last of the fire fizzled into smoke. When Hannes came down from the roof at last, she put both hands on her stomach and took a deep breath.

It's getting late. I must go home. She turned around and began the walk home. Suddenly, Milo appeared beside her. He fell in step without a word. *That is just like him.* They walked in silence, not looking at each other until they reached the lane. At last Milo said, "I'm glad no one was hurt. I think Hannes took home burned pieces of mail. There was a whole big can of burned mail. I looked for a letter from my aunt, but she gets someone to write for her, so I didn't recognize any handwriting."

"Maybe Hannes will find some mail for you," said Elisabeth.

"Yes, maybe he will," agreed Milo.

Elisabeth looked at Milo at last. His hair and long dark eyelashes were singed into powdery feathers on the ends. His face was black with soot and one arm was burnt.

"Milo, you're burnt!" cried Elisabeth.

"Only a little," said Milo.

"Mama keeps some unsalted butter for burns. Come in and I'll get you some."

Milo came in the house while Elisabeth went to the cellar for the butter. She returned and taking a generous gob in her hand, she rubbed it gently onto the burn on his arm. When she had finished she said softly, "There, now it should soon feel better."

"It does already," said Milo. His cheeks blushed pink.

Elisabeth felt her own face burn. *Rubbing Milo's arm made me feel—feel—close to Milo. I'm not sure I like that feeling.*

Abruptly she said, "See you tomorrow," and opened the door for him to leave.

10

The Smell of Smoke

The Thursday after the fire, Elisabeth walked to work at the print shop. A smoky smell assaulted her nostrils as she pushed open the door.

Hannes was bent over the table, intent on scraps of curled, brown paper. He pushed several pieces onto a clean sheet of paper. "Come, help me!" he said.

"Whatever are you doing, Hannes?"

"I picked up the scorched mail they threw out. I'm trying to sort the pages for people so they can read their mail. People will really be grateful if we can save some of it for them, especially those with mail from the motherland. I'm looking for mail from my own mother."

"You have a mother, Hannes?" she asked, surprised, then blushed and said, "Of course, you have a mother!"

"I have a mother for sure," Hannes replied

with a big grin. He rubbed the soft blonde stubble on his chin and scrunched up his blue eyes until they danced with merriment. "Her name is Margaret Anne Weaver and she lives in Langendorf. I also have a brother and two sisters, but no father—he's dead. And I have three cows, two sheep, a horse, ten chickens, and—"

"That's enough!" exclaimed Elisabeth, raising her arms so that her sleeves fell back and her hands spoke for her. She waved away his words and said eagerly, "Can your mother read? Does she want to come to America?"

Elisabeth abruptly stopped her questions when she saw a shadow of sadness go over his face.

"My mother cannot read or write, so she can only ask someone to write for her. I miss her letters greatly. She cannot write from her heart, but tells only of the weather and neighborhood gossip. I long for her to speak to me as in the old days."

When he paused, Elisabeth prompted, "And coming to America?"

"I am saving money to send for her, but it will be a long time yet and she is not well."

His face was filled with a quiet grief. He turned away from her, but not quickly enough to entirely hide eyes brimming with tears.

A long silence fell between them. They sorted pages quietly, fingers deftly moving across the table, minds numb with internal thoughts. Her hands brushed his, and she felt her cheeks flush with pink.

Elisabeth said, "Milo said you brought mail home. He was hoping for a letter from his aunt."

"I'll look especially for it," said Hannes. "Milo seems like a nice boy."

"He's not a boy," said Elisabeth. She felt angry, as though Hannes had taken away some of Milo's dignity. Looking at Hannes, she realized that Milo did indeed seem much younger. His tan cheeks hadn't a shadow of a beard yet and Hannes had a downy fuzz of blonde hair on his chin. She was sure he shaved it off frequently.

"You should do your work now," Hannes chided at last. He pushed the sorted papers out of the way.

Elisabeth was deep in thought. *If I were a mother in Germany, I'd want to write to my own son. If I don't learn to read, I may be all alone somewhere — captured by Indians, or traveling on a train, or sick in bed — and unable to write a letter. Yes, I must not only learn to read, but to write well, no matter how hard it is. I will try harder this week.*

"How do you write 'read'?" she blurted out, then added, "How do you write: 'I want to learn to read and write'?"

Hannes wrote the sentence on a scrap of paper, patiently saying each word as he wrote. Elisabeth watched intently. She said, "Why don't *read* and *write* start alike? They sound alike but read starts with *r* and write starts with *w*. Oh well, I just don't understand yet."

"You did it!" yelled Hannes.

"Did what?" asked Elisabeth in confusion.

"You heard the beginning! You heard the words start alike."

"Yes, they start alike and I don't understand why."

"No one understands that," replied Hannes. "English has some letters that don't make any sense at all. You just have to remember them. But if you want a rule, this is it: when w comes in front of r, the w is silent. Can you remember that?"

"Yes!" she said, hopping off the stool. She hummed as she began to fold papers. Later she cleaned so energetically that Hannes said at last, "Will you slow down a little? My mind can't keep up with you."

A second later he gave a shout, "I found a letter from my mother!" He was quiet as he read. Elisabeth moved the broom softly until he looked up and said, "My sister married and I don't know the man she married. My mother is better and my brother is learning to read English from someone in the village."

Later, as she walked home, Elisabeth made up a tune. She sang, "W before r can't make a sound, make a sound, make a sound. W before r can't make a sound. Wra, wra, wra, wra, wra!"

Her long skirts swirled up dust, but she skipped to the tune she was making in her head. She knew she'd be able to remember the rule now because she had made music of it.

Why must I make music of everything before I can remember it?

Then she remembered that she would have disappointing news for Milo. They hadn't found any letters for him.

Milo met her in the barnyard. "Any letters?" he asked.

She wiped the eagerness from his face with a shake of her head. "No," she said. She felt sad to think that Milo was in America without a single family member being present. She must remember to talk to him more.

11

Compromise

It was nearly dark outside. Elisabeth knelt in the greenhouse, stroking Angelface. The cat arched her back and slid her body back and forth against Elisabeth's hand. Elisabeth spoke softly to her. "Angelface, I want that black velvet and black lace to make my new bonnet, but Papa thinks they're too fancy. If I have to have a plain, ordinary bonnet, I don't want a new one at all. I didn't think Papa would care if I bought it myself. Now Mr. Burger has paid me and Papa doesn't want me to buy that velvet."

"Ummm!" She heard a sound behind her. She turned.

"Milo! Were you listening?" she cried in dismay.

"I couldn't help it," he said. "I was tending these plants and you began talking right in front of me."

"I'm sorry I didn't see you there. I—did you hear what I said?"

"Yes, I'm afraid I did. You want a black velvet bonnet with lace. I don't see anything wrong with that."

"Oh, Milo! I do so want a nice bonnet! How can I convince Papa?"

"I don't know if you can convince your Papa. Maybe you'll have to compromise."

"How?" she asked.

"Maybe he would let you have the velvet without the lace or the lace without the velvet. Compromise means you'll give up something to get part of what you want. Actually, you should have—I'd better not say it."

"Say what, Milo?"

"I'll give you an idea if you don't tell a soul." Elisabeth nodded affirmatively. "Talk to your Papa about a fancier bonnet than the one you had in mind. Then you can give up something that's not really important to you anyway."

"Milo!" Her voice held shock and astonishment. She fell silent, thinking about what he said. She barely heard Milo tap the small tool he was using against the wooden board that held the soil in place in the greenhouse. He dropped the clean tool in the bucket by his side, then stood to his feet.

"It's time for supper," said Milo.

Milo walked her to her house. Tonight was an evening that Mama had made dinner for Milo, too. She sometimes did this to give Grandma Katie a rest. As she washed for supper, Elisabeth was deep in thought. *Milo does have*

an idea that will work. . . . I'll try it out at supper.
But it doesn't seem quite honest.

At the supper table Elisabeth said, "Mama, I asked Papa if I may buy velvet and lace to make a new bonnet. I had in mind wide satin ribbon ties. A deep blue would be nice, but. . . ." She made her voice trail off in a wistful sound.

Papa blurted out, "A deep blue! You didn't ask about a deep blue. I only thought of black. Mama, what do you think? Shall we let Elisabeth buy velvet for a new bonnet?"

"I think it wouldn't hurt, Papa," replied Mama.

"You may buy velvet, but it must be black. How about lace, Mama?"

"Lace? Elisabeth could tat her own lace from black thread. But no wide satin ribbons. Narrow satin, perhaps."

"Narrow satin ribbons, black velvet and . . . I think lace is too *weltlich*." Papa was thoughtful.

Elisabeth interrupted by saying, "I could use that new pattern—"

Papa quickly said, "You may have the lace, but only black and only hand tatted. No new pattern. No, your bonnet shall be made over the old pattern so you look like you belong to this family."

"Oh, thank you, Papa. The black tatting will make a fine edge. It won't be gaudy, I promise you."

"Ummmm!" Milo cleared his throat again. Elisabeth looked at him. She was sure his voice was a signal to her that he knew she had followed his advice. She wrinkled her nose at him when Papa wasn't looking, but Milo only looked frightened. She changed her mind and decided Milo had a throat condition. She suddenly became aware of his flushed cheeks.

After dinner, she followed him into the hall. "Milo." Her voice had a command for him to stop. He turned toward her. "Milo," she repeated, "do you have a sore throat or fever? Tell me why you keep clearing your throat."

"A little sore throat. Nothing much," he said.

"Let me feel your head," she insisted.

He ducked his head to the side, but not quickly enough to altogether escape her touch. His forehead felt hot and dry to her fingers. She knew instantly that Milo was sick. A shiver of dread passed over her. There were so many illnesses that ended in death! She wished there were cures for all of them.

"Milo, you must tell Papa. If you don't, I will."

"It's only a little fever," he protested.

"A little fever could turn into flu, or small pox, or scarlet fever, or tuberculosis, or . . . Oh, Papa!" she exclaimed as her father came into the hall. "Milo has a fever!"

"I can work like always," protested Milo.

"We will see if you are better in the morning," said Papa.

Milo left immediately for Grandma Katie's house. When he had gone, Elisabeth could not shake off the fear that filled her. As she and

Barbara washed supper dishes, Barbara asked, "What will happen if Milo gets real sick? Will he die like Willie Burgess?"

Willie Burgess had been in Barbara's class in school and had died of a fever just the year before. Now Elisabeth said, "Oh, no! I don't think so." Then she was afraid she had lied to Barbara.

The dishes clattered in the pan. Barbara was silent. At last, Elisabeth could stand it no longer. "We had better pray for Milo," she said.

12

Medicine for Milo

Milo came to Elisabeth's house in the morning. Papa took one look at his flushed face and forbade him to go to the barn. Then Papa turned to Elisabeth and said, "I think you are needed to go to the village this morning. Take the butter and eggs to the store and trade them for sugar for Mama and some cough syrup, too. Oh, stop and get some of young Mark Hostetler's Stomach Bitters just in case."

"Papa, I thought you said Mark Hostetler was too young to make medicine," said Elisabeth. "You said Mark should stick to farming, didn't you?"

"I did, but I got some medicine and it helped my cow," said Papa, grinning sheepishly

"So that's what made Mazie better!" Elisabeth's laughter rang out and Papa's hearty chuckle joined in. Even Milo laughed heartily, although he was sitting down to rest in the rocking chair.

Papa said, "Oh, I've been thinking about your reading and about the things women might need to read. You may stop at Mr. Burger's print shop and get Hannes to write you a new sentence, but don't stay long."

Papa tells me Hannes may write a new sentence! Give me a new lesson? Why?

As Elisabeth walked down the road, she puzzled over the change in Papa's attitude. What had happened to him? He said he had been thinking about when women might read. She would have to think about that herself.

In town, she went straight to the store that had been rebuilt since the fire by a store-raising much like a barn-raising. She turned in the eggs and butter for a few coins, then did Mama's shopping for her. She checked on the mail in the post office in the corner of the store. The mail was sorted into a variety of kitchen pans. She wondered how long it would be before the post office had little wooden doors and boxes again.

No mail! The familiar pang of disappointment flew through her. Leaving the store, she walked quickly to Hostetler's.

There she found Mark working in the basement shop he had claimed as his own.

"I want some of your Stomach Bitters," she said.

"Who is sick at your house?" asked Mark.

"It's Milo this time," said Elisabeth.

"Milo? Your new man? Milo looks tough as whale bone. Doesn't have a bit of meat on his bones. But he'll recover. Just have him be careful of the night air. That night air gets to the best of us."

Elisabeth watched Mark measure out the medicine into a small bottle. He measured the doses with precision. At last he put a cork in the bottleneck and glued directions on the side, then wrapped the bottle in brown paper. Elisabeth tucked it in a pocket in the side of her skirt. Stepping outside, she nearly ran into a man who was babbling loudly about the drink he held in his fist.

"Best corn whiskey, sealed with a corn cob in a green gla*sh* jar, ready for your exzhamination. Made by Hiram Elgin. Have a drink now and pay later. Come and get it, folks! Just twenty-five cents a drink."

Elisabeth sniffed the rotten smell that came from his clothes. *Phew! How can he stand to smell his own smell?* She was glad that her father didn't drink. She hurried to the buggy, eager to leave the drunk behind.

As she left, a cool summer rain began to fall. She was glad that Milo was not with her, for the dampness seeped through her clothes until she shivered. On an impulse, she pulled the buggy to the side of the road outside of town, bowed her head and prayed. *Oh God, heal Milo. Don't let him have come all the way across the ocean only to die of sickness when he is safely here.* She stopped and considered, then added, *God, I'm really counting on you.* Then she clucked to the horse and set out briskly for home, her heart light and her spirit lifted. By the time she got home she was singing a song that she had recently learned, *Gott is de liebe.*

She took the medicine to Grandma's house when she got home. Grandma met her at the door. "Milo's very sick. Did you get the medicine?"

"Yes." She pulled the bottle from her skirt.

Grandma took a spoon from the kitchen along into the front room where Milo lay in bed. He talked to them in feverish delirium, "I heard an angel singing about God's love. The song was coming in the window."

"That was Elisabeth singing," said Grandma. But Milo was too fretful to listen.

Elisabeth wished she could sing like an angel. For a moment she wondered if angels sang in German or English, but decided they must have a special heavenly language. She thought Milo would be surprised when he recovered and learned that it had only been Elisabeth singing.

Grandma Katie looked at the words Mark Hostetler had written on the bottle of medicine. Then she shook her head. At last she said, "Elisabeth, go get Katerina. I am afraid I will not get the dose right. And what does it say under the dose?"

As Elisabeth hurried across the yard to the big house, she remembered that Papa had said to stop and get another sentence from Hannes.

Too late, but I'm not sorry I came straight home to get the medicine to Milo. Milo is more important than any sentence I might have got from Hannes. More important than reading.

Then she had a sudden realization. *That's not true! Reading is important. That's why Grandma needs Katerina—to read for her so she gets the dose right. Reading is important to keeping Milo alive.*

13

Caring for Milo

The next week passed quickly. Mama sent Elisabeth to help Grandma nurse Milo as often as she could be spared. Grandma was getting tired from watching him day and night. By Saturday night, she was completely exhausted. Mama and Elisabeth came over from the big house to say Elisabeth could stay with Milo all night.

"No," said Grandma, "but I would take your offer to stay until midnight."

Elisabeth went home to get her needlework to while away the time. When she arrived back at Grandma's half an hour later Grandma was ready for bed.

"I'm going to get a real sleep," Grandma said. "Call me if you need me." She went up to bed, although it was only five o'clock in the afternoon. She left a cold supper on the table for Grandpa Daniel, and Elisabeth.

Milo was fretful. He moaned softly and turned from side to side, but seemed unable to get comfortable. His eyes were closed and though Elisabeth spoke to him, he would not answer. She finally turned away from him, ready to do something else, and determined not to pay attention to him unless he got awake and spoke.

While she watched Milo, Elisabeth was making a woven linen towel embroidered with cross-stitch for her namesake, her little cousin Elisabeth who was only a little over a year old. She threaded her needle with red thread, it seemed for the fiftieth time.

When Milo finally rolled over, she lay her embroidery down and picked up the towel in the basin of cool water and wrung it out. Placing it on Milo's head, she said a silent prayer for his recovery. Again, as when she was driving home yesterday, she felt calm and serene, even joyful. The words of Jesus went through her head, "My peace I leave with you."

While the towel rested on his head, she went to the window and looked out over the lawns. How she loved Grandma's flower beds, the round circles of green leaves with brightly colored flowers in the center! The smell of roses came in the window, sweet with a scent that would make rose jelly if Grandma had time to make it. Elisabeth could see the molded pale pink jelly in her mind. Thinking of eating it with fresh churned butter on homemade bread made her almost drool.

Her thoughts went to Hannes. She had not been to the print shop for a lesson since Milo had been sick. Milo. Hannes. She liked them both. Hannes was laughing and fun, but a tease. So far, Milo was gentle and sober, but would he be like that if he were well? Ach! She didn't need to worry about that. She was only sixteen. Yet, reason told her it was better to be interested in a husband before Mama and Papa began to hint about someone. Her cousin, Virginia, was seventeen and eager to marry Anthony Spears. Elisabeth thought it would be nice to be in love like Virginia.

The sun was making gold streaks across the sky. It sank, a flaming ball, below the hill. When it disappeared, Elisabeth turned around, took the cloth from Milo's head, and dipped it in the cool water. Wringing it out, she replaced it on his head.

When complete darkness came, she lit the oil lamp, but the lamplight soon made her eyes ache. She looked up to see Milo staring at her. It was a vacant stare brought on by the fever. She sat down in the rocker, preparing herself to sit with him until midnight, as she had promised. She picked up her embroidery again, thinking of Baby Elisabeth, her Uncle Samuel's youngest child. She was such a pretty baby with blond curly hair. It was the custom for young girls to make a linen embroidery for a baby named for them. She wished her great-aunt Elisabeth, who lived in Germany, had made something for her, but Germany was so far away. Even if she had made someething, it was probably too expensive to send.

The clock Grandma had moved into the room ticked steadily. At ten o'clock, Elisabeth folded up her embroidery and turned the lamp down to a soft glow. Suddenly, she noticed that Milo looked like he was resting and peaceful. She felt his head. It felt cool. His eyes opened and he smiled.

"*Guten Tag*, Elisabeth!" he said.

"It is night, Milo! I am so glad you are better!"

"*Ich bin in Amerika*?" asked Milo.

"*Ja! Du bist!*" said Elisabeth.

"I dreamed I was on the ship in a storm. The ship slid up the waves—we were on a mountain of water, then the ship slowly rolled over and sank down into a deep valley and the sky disappeared. We were all thrown to one side. We held on and up we would go again into the clouds. Then the bottom would slide sideways under us—we'd go down, down, down into the depths. We would all fall to the other side. There would be screaming and crying. Then water would splash over the side of the boat and into the hold. Sometimes someone would be washed into the water. Then up again. That's what I have been dreaming of for days. Ever since I got this fever. But I am better now. I know it!"

"Oh, Milo! It must have been awful to be at sea in a storm!"

For the next hour, Milo talked softly, telling

Elisabeth about the trip to America. At last, Elisabeth asked a question she had been thinking of asking for days. "Milo, can you read English?"

"No, I can't. Why do you ask?"

"I can't much, either. Hannes Weaver is teaching me."

"Where did Hannes Weaver learn?" asked Milo.

"I don't know," replied Elisabeth, surprised. "I didn't ask him. Why didn't I think to ask that before?"

"I want to learn, too!" said Milo. "Will you teach me what you know?"

"I'll be glad to teach you! But for now, you better rest. We have talked long enough. Hush!" Elisabeth smoothed his dark hair back from his forehead with one hand and leaned on her elbow with the other. She hummed softly. He shut his eyes.

"Do you love Hannes Weaver?" Milo asked the sudden question in a weak voice without opening his eyes.

"No, I don't—I—why do you ask?"

"Good."

He fell asleep. Elisabeth sat alone by his bed, wondering if she had lied to him. She didn't know. The windmill inside her was upside down and stalled. The words were speaking over and over in her head. *Do you love Hannes Weaver? Do you love Hannes Weaver?* She didn't know. She honestly didn't know.

14

Finding Out

August rainfall was perfect. The orchard was polka-dotted with nearly ripe red apples. When Elisabeth walked through tall alfalfa ready for a second cutting of hay, the lush grass tangled and nearly tripped her.

Evenings were warm and pleasant. Elisabeth and Milo often took an oil lamp to the front porch to work on reading together. Elisabeth would practice her lesson and Milo would repeat it. Sometimes, Elisabeth would daydream about Milo as he read his lesson aloud. She would imagine that he smiled and teased like Hannes, but he never did. He was always sober, but she noticed that his face was becoming rounded and his cheeks had a ruddy glow and sometimes he even seemed to relax a bit. Katerina, a good reader, often sat on the porch floor at the edge of the porch. She was moody and listened without comment.

Elisabeth was over her humiliation of having Hannes find her barefoot and took pleasure in the freshly cut lawns that tickled underfoot. By now she could write *Deer Park Farm* and was eager to make her sign. She searched the upstairs of the barn one afternoon, looking again for a piece of board that would make a sign good enough for their farm.

As she came near the hole in the barn floor where they threw down hay for the cows, she heard her little sisters, Barbara and Maria, playing with new kittens in the barn below. Barbara was saying, "I wish Katerina was nice like Elisabeth. Katerina's grumpy."

Maria responded, "Yes, but Elisabeth does get to do more things than Katerina. She goes for reading lessons. I'm going to learn to read so I don't have to go for reading lessons. I work real hard in school."

"Yes, but you don't have to stay home and take care of babies like Elisabeth did." Barbara giggled suddenly, then added, "Besides, I think it would be nice to go for lessons with Hannes. I like Hannes."

Maria made soft sounds to the kitten she was holding. Elisabeth looked down the hay hole and saw the bright red curls of the little girl. Beside her, the mother cat was strutting back and forth. Elisabeth spoke to her little sisters, "Hi, down there!"

"Elisabeth, what are you doing up there?" asked Barbara.

"Trying to find a board to make our new farm sign," replied Elisabeth.

"We're coming up!" said Barbara. In a minute, the two girls had walked outside the barn and appeared on the barn floor. Before they had time to speak, Papa appeared too.

"I heard you wishing for a board for the farm sign," said Papa. "I had one specially cut the other day. It's in the buggy shed, right where I left it when I came home. You'll need to paint it."

"Oh Papa, thank you!" Elisabeth was delighted.

Fifteen minutes later, Elisabeth had the board in the cellar, painting it with the white paint Papa had brought home. Katerina came by and said, "You get picked to paint the sign. I can make letters better than you and I don't get picked."

Katerina disappeared upstairs. Elisabeth told herself not to worry about her sister's comments. *Katerina is irritable. She does not like it that Mama gives me so much freedom and responsibility. Mama is always asking me to do the extra things, like taking care of Milo. That's because I know how to do all the ordinary things. Katerina has always avoided daily work. Now she finds such work unpleasant.*

Katerina was indeed irritable. Then one day, Elisabeth discovered the source of her irritation. She saw Katerina blush when she mentioned Milo. Suddenly, the thought flashed through her head that Katerina might be in love with

Milo. After all, Katerina was fourteen and looked as grown up as Elisabeth.

Elisabeth said to her, "Katerina, you like Milo, don't you?" Remembering Grandma's kind words to her about Hannes, Elisabeth said softly, "Your face betrays you, but your secret is safe with me. I won't mention it to anyone. And I don't love Milo."

She was sure that she didn't love Milo. He was her friend. On the evening Milo's fever broke, he had begun to confide in her. Since then, he had told her many things he had learned about immigrants. Grandma Katie and Grandpa Daniel had given him a better contract than that held by most indentured servants. He had only five years to work for them. He wasn't forbidden to marry as were most servants. And he would be taught the greenhouse business and be given five acres of land at the end of five years. This was because his mother had negotiated a special contract for him before her death. It was also because Elisabeth's grandparents believed in treating Milo as a person, not a slave.

Last week, Elisabeth had sent word with Papa to Hannes that she couldn't come to work on Thursday. Now it was Thursday again. She was eager to go to work and eager for another reading lesson. She saddled up Jingles and climbed into the sidesaddle. She cantered out the lane. At the end of the lane she stopped by the rail fence, pulled up her long skirts, and swung one leg across the horse. Sitting straight in the saddle she galloped almost to the print shop. Then she stopped again, and reseating herself, rode to the shop in the sidesaddle. She was pleased with herself for galloping like the men for a short way, although no one had seen her. She straightened her skirts just before getting there.

"Ho, ho, ho!" Hannes exaggerated his laugh! He had seen her coming and strode onto the front porch to greet her. She allowed him to give her a hand down from the horse and tie it to the railing at the side of the building. She smiled to herself as she thought of how she had galloped to get there! And now Hannes was helping her!

"Hannes, it has been a long time since my last lesson, but I have studied hard. Today I want to do my work first, so I'll get busy right away." Elisabeth pushed up her sleeves. Her plain purple dress with its slim waist showed how strong and limber she was as she bustled about the room, sweeping and gathering up waste paper.

Once, she whirled around. In a flash, she saw Hannes's raised eyes observing her from his bowed head. He lowered his eyes. She had seen a serious contemplating look on his face. What could he be thinking? She couldn't imagine.

"So Milo was sick, was he?" asked Hannes.

"Yes. He was very sick for a while. He was delirious. He talked about his trip over here on the ship. He had to climb the ropes."

"I wished I could climb the ropes. I had only a space about six feet big to live in. I don't want to think about my trip over. It was too awful!"

"Hannes, how did you learn to read?" At last she asked the question that haunted her.

"Mr. Burger taught me. I came over when I was sixteen. I was an angry defiant boy, so men were not bidding on me. Then Mr. Burger came along and he saw something worthwhile in me. Mr. Burger bought my contract from the ship master to end in the year I am twenty-five, but the terms of the contract said he would teach me to read. So that was the first and best thing he did. I began to feel better about myself. And then I knew I was worth something to Mr. Burger."

"He taught you to read when you were sixteen?"

"I was really seventeen before I learned. Then Mr. Burger taught me many other things. He still teaches me. I guess he'll teach me for three more years."

"So you are not free yet?"

"I'm only twenty-two."

"Three more years. . . ." Elisabeth tried to comprehend.

"Mr. Burger is like my family. So is Mrs. Burger, and the boys."

"But you had to give up your mother."

"Mr. Burger promised me he would bring my mother to America if I work until I am twenty-five. It's not in my contract. I just have to trust. And I'm saving my money."

"Milo has only five years to work and you had nine. That doesn't seem fair."

"No, it doesn't seem fair. But think of it this way. Sixteen is a young age. I was really a boy yet. I should have been paying Mr. Burger to learn, so those first years don't count much. Then I start counting the years around twenty. It's only fair I work several extra years—to pay for the reading lessons, ciphering lessons, and handwriting. Oh, and for my apprenticeship at the print shop, too."

Elisabeth was beginning to understand.

Hannes continued on, "Every person is different. Every contract is different. Mr. Burger has to give me a new suit of clothes when I am finished because it's in my contract."

"What other things are in the contracts? Not yours, but a woman's contract?" asked Elisabeth.

"Housewifery, sewing, knitting, spinning. Reading the Bible. Twelve months of school. Sometimes, the contract even says the servants must be healthy. If they aren't healthy, they must stay on board the ship until someone buys their contract. No one wants to buy it, so often they die on the ship."

Elisabeth shivered. "Grandma Katie and Grandpa paid their own way, I think. I'm glad Grandma Katie came to America and not me," she said. Then she felt guilty for having thought it.

15

Invitation to the Social

Elisabeth had come home from the print shop with a new sentence. She was delighted to see how easy the words were to learn. She had them thoroughly memorized by the next day. As she did the washing that morning, she felt a thrill of pleasure as she thought about reading. *It's getting easier every week. I think I will be able to read words I don't know very soon now.*

After the washing was done, Elisabeth got out the fine brush and the black paint and repainted the letters on the farm sign. The repainting and touch-up finished, she cleaned her brush in paint thinner, then washed it with soap and water.

She had just put away her paints when she heard someone speaking to Papa in the front lawn: ". . . and take them to the box social."

Elisabeth felt her face grow hot. Then she heard Papa's voice, too low to understand until the end when she caught a few words, ". . . do not want her to marry . . ."

The voice again. ". . . just wanted them to have a good time. Alice and Sarah will go and who knows who will buy Lizzie's box and eat with her. You know it will go for a good cause."

The word "Lizzie" told her who the speaker was. It was Noah Otto. Noah had called her Lizzie in school. But now she was not in school and seldom saw Noah. Only Hannes sometimes called her Lizzie besides Noah.

Elisabeth knew what a box social was. Every girl packed a meal for two, then decorated the container. At the box social, the box was auctioned off to the highest bidder, who ate with the young lady who had decorated his purchase.

Now she wondered what Noah was talking about. Again, she heard Papa say, "I know a school is needed, but I can't allow my girls to . . . "

Elisabeth ran to the side of the house. She couldn't be seen here, but neither could she hear any more of the conversation. *Oh, Papa, I'm so embarrassed! I can't believe that you would tell Noah that you don't want us to associate with him. But I can believe it. I have known all my life that you expect me to marry someone like—like—like Milo. I want to go to the social. It would be such fun to decorate a box. I don't want to find a husband. I just want to have fun.* A pang of keen disappointment went through her. She dropped to her knees and began weeding a flowerbed. She weeded rapidly until she had finished the whole bed. Then she went in the house.

Papa was inside. Elisabeth was so curious she fairly itched to ask Papa, but he didn't mention his visitor and she didn't ask.

All that day and the next she stewed about Noah's visit. Then, on the third day, when the whole family was there at dinner, Papa brought it up. "I had a visit from Noah Otto," he said. "He asked if I would let my two girls go with him and his sisters to the box social. They are trying to make money to build the new school. I didn't want to let you girls go at first, but I've been thinking that he didn't ask for either of you. It was like a family invitation. Then I heard the minister was letting his girls go. So, Elisabeth and Katerina, you may go with Noah and his sisters. Noah's coming back tonight to get your answer, so you decide and let me know."

"We want to go!" said Elisabeth and Katerina together.

After dinner, Katerina said to Elisabeth, "Milo might like to go too."

"He hasn't any money to buy a box," said Elisabeth. "Besides, he's too shy. I don't think he'd go even if he had the money."

"I know, but I can wish, can't I?" asked Katerina.

"Ye-e-e-s," said Elisabeth slowly, "maybe Grandpa would give him money."

"You ask," said Katerina, but Elisabeth wouldn't ask and neither would Katerina.

Elisabeth heard Katerina tell Milo about the social and hint that she'd like to go with him, but he did not respond. Milo seemed to withdraw and become quieter as the time came nearer for the social.

There were two weeks until the box social. Elisabeth had decided to wear her new bonnet to the social for the first time. She had already tatted a tiny edge of black lace to go around the front of it. She went into the village the next time she went to work at the print shop and bought the black velvet. Aunt Maria had the pattern and she would make it for her.

On the way home, she touched the black velvet over and over. It was so soft! She had never had a velvet bonnet before—always a stiff black plain fabric. She rubbed it against her cheek. She could hardly wait for the bonnet to be done. She hoped that the weather did not turn to a hot Indian summer when velvet would not be appropriate to wear to the social.

That evening she held the velvet up to her face and looked in the mirror. She was pleased at her reflection. Her white skin looked smooth and soft against the fabric. Her cheeks had a hint of color and her lips were moist and rosy. Against the blackness, her eyes, usually gray-blue, looked deep and aquamarine with long dark lashes.

As she drove to Aunt Maria's house on Friday morning, she thought about the box social. *Will Hannes be there? Who will he take to the social?*

Will Hannes like my bonnet? Then she berated herself. *Why do I always think of Hannes? Papa will never let me marry him. If I want to marry Hannes, I will have to wait until I am old — at least eighteen — and go against Papa's will.*

She drove in the lane to Aunt Maria's house. Uncle Louis had built it for their family when he and Maria moved out of the house where Elisabeth and her family now lived. Elisabeth admired the neat white house. Then the door burst open and three small boys appeared to smile shyly at her from the yard gate. They were Maria's grandchildren. Maria came to the door.

"Oh, Elisabeth, what lovely material for the bonnet!"

"Could you get it done for the box social?" asked Elisabeth.

"I'll surely try. Let's fit the pattern to your head." Maria bustled into the dining room where she kept her sewing and Elisabeth followed.

Maria was busy sewing all day. By the time evening came, Elisabeth's bonnet was completely finished. When she put it on, her skin looked creamy white against the black velvet and her eyes were large and luminous. She looked at herself in the mirror, whirled slowly around and around, then clapped her hands with delight.

Elisabeth couldn't have been more pleased with the way the bonnet was made. There was an edge of narrow black lace around the brim of the bonnet, so narrow it could scarcely be seen.

And the bonnet tied under the chin with narrow satin ribbon.

"This bonnet is just right for me," she said.

"It surely is!" exclaimed Maria. She picked up one of the crying grandchildren and set her on her hip, then added, "You are growing into a real beauty. I was surprised to hear you are going with Noah, though. I thought you'd go with Hannes."

Elisabeth answered shyly, "I don't think Hannes is for me. We are always arguing and fussing."

Maria smiled and said, "Fire goes out for lack of fuel."

"What do you mean?" asked Elisabeth.

"Think about it."

Fire goes out for lack of fuel. Let's see. The upside down would be that fire burns because of fuel. What kind of fire does she mean? Love? Surely not! Arguing and fussing can't make love grow. The windmill is turning again. The words are going round and round and I can't tell what is true! I will just remember what Aunt Maria said. Fire goes out for lack of fuel. Someday the meaning will become clear.

16

Elisabeth Gets a Test

The social was on Friday evening and Elisabeth worked at the print shop on Thursday. She was dying to know if Hannes was going, but he was in a teasing mood and didn't want to talk about anything serious.

First of all, he had decided to give her a test. He had written a note. Now he teased her that she couldn't read it aloud. She stuffed it in her pocket and said, "When I am finished with my work, I will read it."

"Oh, ho! The lady delays," teased Hannes.

"I'm not delaying. I'm just waiting until my work is done so I can concentrate on what I am reading."

"Oh! The lady wants to concentrate!" he teased.

"Well, I do! Is anything wrong with that?" she asked.

"Not a thing, Ma'am. Not a thing!"

Elisabeth looked at his dancing blue eyes. He made her so frustrated! Aloud, she asked, "Why do you want me to take this test?"

"Because I want to see what you do alone. I want you to have to struggle with those sentences. Next week, I'll give you a writing test—see if you know the upside down."

She dawdled with her work. She knew she was delaying, but she couldn't seem to hurry. When she pulled out the note at last, she was aghast when she saw it. She felt as she had felt when she had been asked to recite in school. All rational thought fled. Raw fear remained. Although Elisabeth couldn't read it, the note said:

Elisabeth, go to a greenhouse and get me a carrot, a bean, a flower, and a cucumber. Put them in a pan and bring them to me. Hannes

She looked at it with blind, unseeing eyes. After a bit she said, "I can't read it yet. May I take it along home and think about it."

"If you talk to no one about it. Promise?"

"I promise."

"This is all the lesson you will have. Go home and read your other lessons and think about them." His voice was sober now, without any of the teasing overtones that had been there a short time before. He turned back to his work and ignored her. She left, feeling crushed. He had put all daydreams of having a good time with him at the social out of her head. Suddenly, she wasn't looking forward to going anymore.

All evening she moped, not playing games with Milo and Katerina and refusing to help Milo with his reading as she had been doing frequently. She also refused to look at her note. She knew she was doing exactly as she had done when a child. She was blocking reading out of her life. By bedtime, she had persuaded herself that the sensible thing to do was ignore the note until after the box social. She put it in a dish in the dresser drawer and shut it out of her mind.

17

Hannes Buys a Box

Elisabeth had intended to ask Hannes if he was going to the social, but his test had upset her so that she hadn't asked him. Now it was time to get ready for the social. With Katerina getting ready too, some of the excitement she had felt returned to her.

She dressed in her best navy blue dress, which accented her eyes. Her narrow high button shoes were getting old and pinched her feet that seemed to have grown the last month, but she would have to wear them anyway. She combed her hair into deep dark waves, as high and curly as she thought Papa would allow. Then she tried on her black shawl and her new bonnet. Splendid! She took them off again to help Katerina with her hair.

Elisabeth thought Katerina looked lovely in her deep wine-colored dress. She piled Katerina's auburn waves high on her head and put a comb in her hair to hold it up. She stepped back and admired her sister. She had just finished with the combing when she heard Noah downstairs.

The two girls rushed down the stairs, slowing from their headlong dash in time to enter the room graciously. Getting ready with Katerina had made Elisabeth feel excitement once again. She would have fun, no matter what happened.

They said their good-byes to Papa and Mama. Elisabeth tried not to notice that Papa's eyebrows had raised as he looked at Katerina. Noah looked at Elisabeth with eyes that recognized her beauty, but Elisabeth ignored his stare. The younger children babbled and chattered in their efforts to get themselves noticed. Jacob and Peter were in the kitchen eating. The two decorated boxes with the dinners to be auctioned rested on the kitchen sideboard.

The two girls gathered up their boxes and walked through the October orange and gold dusk to the buggy. Noah put the boxes in the back of the buggy along with his sisters' boxes. Alice and Sarah were waiting in the buggy. Alice made room for Elisabeth between her and Noah and Sarah moved over on the back seat for Katerina. Elisabeth became uneasy immediately when Noah pushed against her. She moved over against Alice and he didn't follow, but the uneasiness lingered all through the ride to Phillips' barn where the social was being held.

At Phillips' barn, Noah got the boxes out for

the girls. He followed closely on Elisabeth's heels into the building. Once inside, he steered her with a hand on her elbow. *How annoying!*

Just as she placed the box with the others, a familiar wide mouth caught her eye. She saw Hannes looking her way. There was a strange look on his face and he seemed to gaze past her. She turned around to look and saw that he was eyeing Noah. She shook off the annoying hand from her elbow. In a moment, Hannes came over to her and said, "I didn't know you were coming. I didn't think you would be allowed. . . ."

Noah disappeared in the crowd of young people.

"Papa almost didn't let me come, but Noah asked for Katerina and me to come with his sisters and him. Papa said yes at last."

"I . . . I . . . " stuttered Hannes, "I brought Anna Hostetler. If I'd have known. . . ."

Elisabeth felt a sinking feeling in her stomach. "I'm not with anyone. That's the only way Papa would let me come, I am sure."

"I'll see you later," said Hannes. She watched his tall lean body move back through the crowd until she finally saw Anna.

Elisabeth and Katerina found each other and stayed together when the bidding began. When a pretty box decorated with pink came up, Elisabeth saw Hannes bid eagerly. As the price went up, Hannes bid more and more slowly. Finally, Amos Miller bid higher with a loud, triumphant shout, "I'll get your dinner, Anna, so I will." Then he bid one more time, a whole dollar above the last bid.

"Sold to Amos Miller," called the auctioneer.

Amos pushed through the crowd and took his pink and white box. Anna looked close to tears, Elisabeth thought, as Amos took his place at her side.

Finally Elisabeth's box, decorated in navy and light blue, came up for bids. The bidding went fast. Noah was bidding and Elisabeth was sure Noah would buy her box. Then she lost track of who was bidding and how much. When the auctioneer said, "Sold to Hannes Weaver," she was amazed. *How had Hannes managed to bring one girl and eat with another?*

Hannes came forward and got her box, then came back to stand beside her. She felt embarrassed and confused. Her cheeks were hot and she dropped her head. Katerina punched her to say, "Noah got my box."

Hannes, on the other side of her, said, "Lizzie, I wanted to eat with you."

"You tried to buy Anna's." Elisabeth's temper flared.

Hannes leaned down and whispered in her ear, "Don't tell a soul, but I paid Amos a dollar to bid higher than I, so I could bid on your box."

"You didn't!"

"Yes, I did!"

The warmth of knowing Hannes had paid extra to eat with her stayed with her all evening. When at last the auctioning was done, the couples found places around the barn to eat. Hannes found a place on the barn floor that was clean and smooth. Elisabeth sat down on the floor, being careful not to rub her dress on the rough boards. Then Hannes opened the box.

"What's in this box?" asked Hannes as he struggled with the navy fabric tied around it.

"Fried chicken, corn bread with a little jar of maple syrup, potato salad, cake, and fruit salad," she listed.

Hannes opened the top and began to pull out—Elisabeth was aghast. Stones! There were stones inside wrapped up in tea towels.

"What is—?" Hannes stopped in mid-sentence. "Are you playing tricks?"

"No! I packed what I said. Really, I did! My— My—My brothers! They were in the kitchen eating when we left. I thought it was funny they were eating. They giggled when we came in the kitchen. I know they did this. I just know it!"

18

No Dinner

Hannes and Elisabeth were speechless while the enormity of the trick dawned on them. They stared at each other. Elisabeth hadn't eaten all day so she could eat plenty tonight. She was truly hungry. But the box was empty.

"We have no dinner then, do we?" asked Hannes.

"Maybe Katerina and Noah have more than they need," suggested Elisabeth. "Let me ask her."

Before giving him time to answer, Elisabeth was off to find Katerina. Katerina and Noah were outside sitting on a large rock to eat.

"Katerina, we have stones instead of food. I think that Jacob and Peter did this. Do you have extra food?"

"No," said Katerina. "Noah and I just finished eating all of it. We got so hungry we came out and began eating before the auction was done. Now we are finished."

"Oh Katerina, what shall I do? Hannes bought my box for nothing. He already paid!" She clapped her hand over her mouth. She must not betray Hannes's trust in telling her about the dollar he had given Amos.

She picked her way back across the barn floor, treading lightly between laughing and talking couples. At last she reached Hannes and said, "They ate it all. I suppose we'll have to go home to get more food. I don't have any more chicken, but there is potato salad and cake. But you have to take Anna home, don't you?"

"I'll see what I can do about Anna," said Hannes.

He was gone for a few minutes. When he returned, he said to her, "Let's go. Amos will take Anna home. I am hungry, aren't you?" He took her hand and pulled it through his bent arm. He found Katerina and they told her he would be taking Elisabeth home. He led her to the buggy that he had borrowed from Mr. Burger. In a few minutes they were trotting along under a full moon.

They were silent for a while, lost in their own thoughts. Then Hannes said, "I have something to tell you. I am going to be baptized next Sunday."

"Baptized?" Elisabeth was incredulous.

"Yes, I was baptized as a baby in Germany, but I want to be baptized again. I am joining the small church of believers out at Cassel Ridge. They have services in English. I don't want to belong to a church that uses only German. I think that people who speak only English should be able to understand the services."

"The church out at Cassel Ridge is—liberal, Papa says." Elisabeth was hesitant.

"I can live with that. They believe that Jesus is the Savior and that is what's important." His voice was low and even.

Elisabeth turned to see his face in the moonlight. Was this really Hannes speaking? Hannes had religious beliefs that were important to him? She had thought he was a tease and a handsome man, but now she was having to readjust her thoughts.

Hannes continued. "I know I've never talked about religion much, but I am a believer. Are you? Have you been baptized? Do you belong to a church?"

"Yes," said Elisabeth, "I belong to the church my parents belong to, the big meeting house in the village. I was baptized two summers ago. I can't quite believe that you are joining the church at Cassel Ridge. They say the women don't even sit separate from the men there, but they sit in families. Is that true?"

"Yes, it's true!" Hannes slipped into his teasing voice. "What is so wrong with that?"

They were nearly home. Elisabeth could see the light from the oil lamp in the window as they drove up outside the picket fence. Suddenly, she was afraid to take Hannes to the house. What would Papa say when he saw her alone with Hannes? But Hannes was already getting out. He offered her a hand down from the buggy.

She led the way in the walk. Their footsteps were hollow echoes on the porch. She opened the door and stepped inside. There sat Mama quilting and Papa was repairing some harness. Elisabeth spoke in a burst of information, "That Peter and Jacob! They took out the food and put stones in my box. Hannes bought my box. We opened it up and there was no food, only these dish cloths. We are so hungry. I said there was cake and potato salad left at home. May we eat it? Oh, and Hannes brought me home. I could just wring their necks, those boys!"

Her outburst over, Elisabeth looked at Hannes. He stood with his hat in his hand. Then he spoke, "I am sorry about the box, but I didn't mind bringing Elisabeth home."

"You go on to the kitchen with Elisabeth and find something to eat. Never let it be said that I left a guest leave hungry. Now for those boys. Peter! Jacob! Come here!" Papa's voice boomed up the stairs.

As the boys came downstairs, Elisabeth went to the kitchen followed by Hannes. She made a quick trip to the water trough room in the basement where running water kept everything cool. There was only a little cake left. Upstairs, she found the potato salad in the icebox. As they sat there eating, she heard Papa thunder in the next room, "You will not eat any of the things

Mama bakes this week. One week with no cake, no pie! Is that understood?"

Hannes finished the cake and the potato salad. Elisabeth found a piece of the pork roast they had had for dinner and made sandwiches of it. A few canned plums and several stale cookies completed their meal. With the dishes cleaned up, the two of them put on their wraps and sat down on the front porch swing.

A full moon was rising. Hannes put his arm along the back of the swing and his fingers touched her shoulder. Elisabeth felt her teeth begin to chatter from the cold, but also from the nearness to Hannes. Hannes talked quietly for a few minutes. Then he said, "I'd better go since your father didn't want you to date anyone tonight. It's been a great evening. I had a good time."

He stood up, took both her hands in his, and looked into her eyes. "You mean a lot to me," he said softly. Then he turned and was gone.

Elisabeth stood looking after him. Suddenly she heard someone say behind her, "Where's Katerina?"

Turning, she came face to face with Milo. His dark eyes looked deeper than usual. "She's coming home with Noah," she said.

"Oh, I just wondered. Thought I might wait for her, but if she's with Noah, I'd better not."

"Milo, do you like Katerina?"

"She's very beautiful. So are you." Milo turned abruptly and disappeared into the dark.

19

Elisabeth Can Read!

It was a cold November Saturday morning. Elisabeth paused in her scrubbing to read the note that Hannes had said was a test, now getting damp from her wet hands.

Elisabeth, go to the greenhouse and get me a _____, *a* _____, *a* _____, *and a* _____. *Put* _____ *in a pan and br—ing* _____ *to me.*
Hannes

Hannes had said to think about it. She was thinking and nothing was coming of it. She tried again. *Elisabeth, go to the greenhouse and get me a c-c-car—-rr—ot! I got it! Just skip over the letters lightly! That's the way! A carrot! What else shall I get from the greenhouse? A be-beeeeeee-n. A bean! A flo-flo-flow-er. A flower! and a cu-u-u-cum—cucum—ber! a cucumber! Put the-the- I can't get this one. mmm. The-m. Them! Put them in a pan and br-ing them to me. I can read! I CAN READ! I CAN READ!*

"Mama! I can read!" Elisabeth shouted down the stairs. She hugged Barbara and Maria who were playing in the hallway with their dolls. She turned two cartwheels in the hall, then raced downstairs. "Mama, I can read my test note!"

Her mother came running, "Goodness me! Whatever is happening? You can read?"

Elisabeth pulled out her note and read it aloud. Her mother clasped her hands and exclaimed, "Oh, Elisabeth, you really can read! I'm so excited. If you can read, maybe I can learn to read English someday."

"Oh, Mama, may I take these things to Hannes in a pan, like it says? Then he will know I can read."

"You may take them, but come straight back. There is work to be done."

Elisabeth sang to herself as she got a pan from the kitchen, took it to the greenhouse and gathered a carrot, a bean, a flower, and a cucumber. Then she quickly pulled a heavy shawl around her shoulders and scurried out the lane and down the road. At the end of the lane, she paused for a brief moment to admire the sign that said *Deer Park Farm.* She had finished painting it long ago, but Papa had put it up only last week. Then she hurried on.

When she arrived at Mr. Burgers', she saw with dismay that the door to the print shop was closed and there was no smoke coming from the chimney. When she tried the door, it was locked. She was about to go home when she heard a sharp whistle from the orchard. Turning around, she saw Hannes with a saw in his hand. *Pruning apple trees!*

She ran to him, calling, "I can read, Hannes, I can read!" The things in the pan bounced and rattled under the lid. When she reached him, she showed the things she had brought.

"Lizzie, Lizzie, you did it! You can read! You can read! Yew-eeeeeeee!" Hannes danced around and swung by his arms from the apple tree. At last, he stopped his wild joy and stood there grinning. "You don't need me anymore," he said.

"I do, too!" came instantly from her mouth. She couldn't imagine life without Hannes in it. His grin grew even larger.

"I have something for you. I've been saving it for this day. Wait until I get the keys for the print shop and I'll get it for you."

Elisabeth walked back with him to the shop, then waited there on the front porch. Hannes soon came with the key.

"Mr. Burger must trust you a lot," commented Elisabeth as he unlocked the door.

"Like I'm his own son he tells me," said Hannes. Inside, he went to a cupboard in the back of the shop. Opening it, he took something out that looked like a book.

"Here it is." Hannes reverently lifted a book from the shelf and handed it to her. She knew what it was instantly.

The Bible, Elisabeth read from the front. It was a worn book. She opened it.

Hannes was explaining. "I didn't have a Bible when I came here on the ship, but when so many people were dying, it suddenly seemed important to have one. I took care of an old man on the ship and he gave this to me just before he died. Then a year or so ago, I got myself a new Bible. Now I want you to have this one. It was a special gift to me so I want it to be a special gift to you."

Hannes continued on, "Now I want to tell you something else about reading. This is my next lesson. Read this Bible. Pick a chapter, read it, and just skip over the words you don't know. Don't even try to say them. Keep reading the same passage again and again. The words will begin to pop in your head like magic. You will know what they are without even trying. When you can read a whole chapter, come back and read it to me. Don't worry if it takes a long time. Just keep reading it every day and I promise it will work."

"Oh, thank you, Hannes!" replied Elisabeth. "Now I must be going. Mama said I was to come straight back." She pulled her shawl more closely about her, suddenly remembering the night of the box social. Hannes had gone home early. Or at least he had said he was going. She would have liked for him to stay and talk longer, but that was not to be. Elisabeth sighed. If only. . . .

She turned and left the print shop. At the bend in the road, she turned and looked back. Hannes was still on the porch, looking after her. He waved, a tiny figure in the distance.

20

Promises to Keep

There was an ice storm at the end of November. Ice clattering on the greenhouses broke some of the glass. Papa had to go east to get new glass panes. While he was gone, Hannes came to visit Papa in the evening. His face was so grave that Elisabeth wondered if someone had died. She asked him about it as he stood in the hallway. He smiled and said no, no one had died. Then he went back home without telling what he wanted with Papa. Elisabeth did not go for a reading lesson because there was sleet in the air.

The next week he returned again. This time Papa was there. He took Hannes in the parlor and shut the door. The two men were in there a long time. At last Hannes came out, dressed in his outdoor clothes, shook Papa's hand gravely, and said, "I'll see you again next week."

When he was gone, Elisabeth asked Papa, "What did Hannes want?"

"It doesn't concern you now," said Papa. "It is about the future."

"What about the future?" asked Elisabeth. No amount of coaxing could get Papa to reveal any more of their discussion. And when Elisabeth went to the print shop to work, Hannes was sober, not at all like his usual self. He did his work quietly and listened to Elisabeth read, said she was doing well, and dismissed her with a good-bye.

On the third week, Hannes came to the door once again and asked to speak to Papa. He was there only briefly. Then he went off into the cold night, rubbing his hands together briskly. All these conferences that Elisabeth didn't understand made her restless. She wondered if she had said or done anything the night of the social to make Hannes sad.

In the greenhouse, while digging soil to prepare for planting, Elisabeth asked Milo if he knew what Hannes wanted. Milo didn't know. On the fourth week, Hannes came out of the parlor with a smile on his face, followed by Papa who seemed to have relaxed. After Hannes left, Papa smiled and joked with the family, something he hadn't done for a long time.

Elisabeth had chosen a random chapter, Psalms 27, to read every day. Just as Hannes had said, words began to pop in her head. Finally, one day the last verse of the chapter came to her: "Wait on the Lord: be of good courage, and he shall strengthen thine heart: wait, I say, on the Lord."

She was delighted. She was soon able to read the whole chapter, but she didn't get to read it to Hannes right away. The weather had turned blustery and cold and the approaching holiday season left much work to be done.

Christmas came and went, followed by the New Year. Winter set in with a fury of snow and wind. Elisabeth was unable to go to the print shop and Hannes did not come to the house. Milo came down to the "big house" after supper to play games by lamplight. Katerina, and sometimes Peter and Jacob, and Elisabeth played at the kitchen table. Maria and Barbara sometimes played games of their own on the other end of the table. And the babies, Adam and Leah, played on the floor until bedtime, which was early. By 8:30, even the grownups went to bed.

Then came the January thaw at the end of the month. The work at the greenhouses sped up with anticipation of the lettuce and tomato seasons. Finally, on a still white snowy evening, before dusk, a sleigh pulled up to the picket fence. Elisabeth saw it through the greenhouse glass. She went to the packing room door to look out. Hannes was walking to the house. Hannes! How could he come to see Papa and not greet her? She felt the impulse to run to the house, but she restrained herself. Sadly, she went back to work.

She finished transplanting a dozen tomato plants. Then a shadow fell across her hands.

She looked up. Hannes! She jumped to her feet and put out a grimy hand. He took her hand in both of his. He said, "I came to see if I could take you for a sleigh ride. I missed you and your smiling face. I asked your Papa and he said you may go."

"Oh my, I am not dressed to go," she protested.

"I'll wait for you."

She hurriedly finished up in the greenhouse, then rushed to the house. She washed her hands and face and changed her clothes. When she went downstairs, she found Hannes sitting in the parlor, hat on his knee. He smiled and stood up when she came in the room.

"Ready to go?" he asked.

"Ready." Her heart was pounding. What could Hannes want with her? Why was he taking her for a sleigh ride? After weeks of soberly ignoring her, why would he be smiling and attentive now?

The sky was pink in the west as Hannes gave her a hand up to the seat and tucked a robe around her knees. He got in and clucked to the horse. They trotted out the lane. Hannes turned west so they faced the setting sun. Neither of them spoke. At last, the sun sank below the horizon and only the pink and blue of the sunset remained. They were alone, with no houses in sight.

Hannes stopped the horse. He turned to her and said, "It's a cold night, isn't it?" He took another robe from under the seat and wrapped it across her knees and around her legs.

"Yes, it is," she said, her teeth chattering. His arm went around her and pulled her close against him. The sudden warmth of his body through her shawl was unexpected and made her quiver inside. He held her firmly while they watched the evening sky. At last she quit shivering.

He said, "Elisabeth, I have something to tell you. I love you and I'd like to marry you someday." His voice had an anxious sound. She was astonished.

"Oh, Hannes! I haven't thought seriously about marriage. I won't be seventeen until next month. I love you, but Papa will never let me marry you."

"Your Papa will let you marry me. I wanted his blessing, so I came to see him. I have been waiting a long time for him to decide. He wanted you to marry in the church. I said I prayed that you would be my wife. I said I am in the church, but not your congregation. I said the church is a big family of many people, all believers. Finally your Papa said he studied the Bible and he believes I am right. He said he trusts you to do what is right."

"Papa gives you his blessing?" She could hardly believe it. She sat still and felt a great white quietness surround her. Hannes tightened his arm around her shoulder. She felt warm and safe and—loved, but she saw the tension in his face.

Hannes continued, "You see, I can't marry you right now. I am redemptioned for three more years to Mr. Burger. You know redemptioners cannot marry, don't you? But I love you so much. I couldn't bear to think you might marry someone else because I delayed."

She turned toward him. Her eyes met his. She said softly, "I love you, Hannes, and I'd marry you if I had to wait five years—or even ten."

She saw joy go across his face.

"I am so happy!" Hannes put down the reins and hopped out of the sleigh. Then with a joyful roar, he turned into a boy and cartwheeled down the road, right through the deep snow.

"Me, too!" cried Elisabeth. She jumped out of the sleigh and she too, cartwheeled in the road.

"I'm going to marry Hannes! I'm going to marry Hannes!" sang Elisabeth. She cartwheeled over and over again. At last Hannes caught her in his arms and kissed her on the cheek.

She turned to him then and they kissed, a tender, gentle, reverent kiss. She looked deep into his eyes, so blue the lingering light melted them into expressions of his love.

"We must get back," Hannes said. He helped her back in the sleigh, leaped in himself, turned the horse and sleigh around, and they set out for home. Hannes began singing,

And when we come to Baltimore. . . .

Elisabeth joined him.

We'll hold our hands upraised. . . .

When they had sung that song, they began to sing *Gott is die liebe.*

When they reached home, Hannes said, "We will keep this between ourselves, and we will wait to get married for three years. Can we wait so long?"

"We can, Hannes! We can!"

21

The Wedding Preparations

"**T**hree years has been a long time," said Elisabeth. At dusk, she and Katerina sat on the lawn watching the sunset while the last batch of cookies cooled inside. Elisabeth felt contented after the long day of preparing food for the wedding. The women who had come to help had fried several hundred doughnuts and baked thirty dozen cookies. They had divided the fifty chickens and taken them home to fry. They would bring back the broth made into dressing and gravy tomorrow. What an exciting and busy day!

Now Elisabeth watched the windmill turn slowly, silhouetted against the sky. Yes, it had been three years and six months since Hannes had said he loved her, since they cartwheeled down the road through the snow. Hannes was now twenty-five.

"Yes, three years has been a long time," echoed Katerina. "I thought Milo would never notice me. But he finally did, though it took two years!"

Elisabeth knew Milo had liked Katerina long ago. Besides, she wondered how anyone could not notice Katerina. With her auburn wavy hair, she was a beautiful woman, striking in her tall slenderness.

Whoo, whoo.

"Do you hear an owl hooting?" asked Katerina.

The two girls listened, but there was silence except for a cow bawling in the distance.

"Tomorrow is the day!" said Elisabeth. "We talk to the ministers in the morning. Then we go to the meetinghouse for the sermon and the promises. And we come back here for the meal. I am so glad the lawn is full of flowers. Can you smell the moonflowers, Katerina? I can smell them."

She was pleased to know the vines were growing up across the front porch, gracing the whole veranda with the spiral buds and puffed-out parachutes of half-inflated white moonflowers. They would open up for the wedding meal when all the people of the church were expected to come. She hadn't sent invitations, because everyone was invited to the wedding.

The wedding was a sacred service that was meant to be an expression of their faith as well as a solemn commitment. Milo and Katerina and Hannes and Elisabeth would be getting married at the same time—a double wedding.

Katerina leaned against Elisabeth's knee. She said, "Just think! We used to always be fussing at each other. Now we are getting married together. Oh—now I hear that owl again."

Whoo, whoo!

Elisabeth was too full of thought to notice. She smiled to herself. "Yes! And now when we are grown enough to be friends at last, we will be parted. I will be going to live with Hannes in the little house we built by the print shop and you and Milo will be living in the log shed."

Elisabeth and Katerina both giggled. They thought it funny that Katerina would live in the old shed. The two girls and Mama had spent the summer scrubbing and making the shed into a home for Milo and Katerina. At the back of the garden, it now had curtains at the windows and odd furniture inside. Milo had two more years to work for Grandpa, so the two of them planned to live as inexpensively as possible.

"I was so jealous of you," said Katerina. "I thought you would take Milo from me. I loved him from the day he came. And I never thought you would be marrying Hannes."

"Neither did I," said Elisabeth. "I didn't think Papa would permit it. Last night, Papa told me that he kept Hannes waiting for two months while he thought about it. Hannes asked him five times, mind you. Five times!"

"What made Papa decide?" asked Katerina.

125

"When Hannes came the last time to ask, Papa said, 'Why should I give my blessing to your marriage?' Hannes told him, 'See that windmill? I tease a lot but underneath I am like that windmill. Slow and steady and silent. I will take good care of your Elisabeth.' Papa told him he still didn't know.

"But the next morning Papa was reading in the Bible where it says God's spirit is like the wind. Papa said he realized that it was the same spirit—the wind—that moved Hannes although he didn't belong to the same church."

"Papa had a hard time to convince the minister to marry you, didn't he?" asked Katerina.

"Yes, but it helped that you and Milo were getting married at the same time."

It had grown dark while they sat talking.

Whoo, whoo.

"Now I hear an owl!" exclaimed Elisabeth.

Suddenly, there was a burst of sound like a sneeze under the porch. Elisabeth jumped up.

"Come out from there this minute," she commanded, stooping to see under the porch.

Jacob's dark curls appeared first, followed by Peter's straighter hair.

"Look at you! You're almost grown and you're still playing baby tricks!" she scolded.

Jacob and Peter were brushing dirt from their clothes. Jacob said, "Did you hear the owls? Fooled you, didn't we?"

Katerina swatted at them with her hand. "Owls! You are *some owls*!"

The two boys went off together, giggling. Katerina and Elisabeth went inside to pack up the cookies in the big iron kettle with a lid. Elisabeth put a few slices of bread in the kettle on top of the cookies. She knew the bread would be dry and the cookies moist when she opened the lid tomorrow. No mice would get in that kettle. She put the kettle behind the stove on the shelf where cookies were usually put. Then she stood considering. *Peter and Jacob. Can I trust them?*

She took the kettle with the cookies in it, left the kitchen by the back steps, and scurried through the darkness to the greenhouse. There she placed the cookie kettle in the packing house under an overturned barrel. Now it would be safe from Jacob and Peter.

22

The Wedding

After receiving the instructions for marriage from the ministers in the morning, the four young people returned home for lunch, then went back to the church for the afternoon wedding service.

Elisabeth wore a light-blue dress. White dresses were not the custom. She was dressed simply and wore no flowers, as flowers were not permitted in the wedding service. She felt a pang of regret that the church did not let her decorate the church building. People felt that decorations would take away the reverence meant for God and the seriousness of the marriage vows would not be respected. Elisabeth sighed. Sometimes, she could not understand why customs had to be so strict.

Now Elisabeth sat on the front pew with Hannes. Beside her sat Katerina and Milo. On either side of them sat their attendants, two pairs of young people. The sermon had lasted nearly an hour, but it was nearly over. The exhortations were nearly all said.

Elisabeth listened to the minister speak. He was giving his last final practical instructions, spoken in German. "In your marriage, follow these directions from Philippians, the second chapter: In everything you do, stay away from complaining and arguing so that no one can speak a word of blame against you. You are to lead clean innocent lives as children of God in a dark world."

Elisabeth wondered if she would be able to keep from arguing with Hannes. If only he wouldn't tease. When he teased, she always flew into a fluster of protest.

The minister continued, "And turning to Ephesians 4, we read that we should be humble and gentle. Be patient with each other, making allowance for each other's faults because of your love. Try always to be led along together by the Holy Spirit, and so be at peace with one another. Let us remember these words and follow them."

The minister closed his Bible. He came and stood in front of Elisabeth and Hannes and Katerina and Milo. "Those who want to be married, stand," he said.

Elisabeth stood with her mind swirling. *The windmill turns!* she thought. *My mind won't stop spinning. Hannes climbing down from the pine tree. Hannes teaching me to read. Because of*

Hannes, I can take my place with Mama and Grandma Katie in a long line of women going into the past, into Germany. When Hannes and I have children, that line of women will reach into the future. . . .

The minister was asking Hannes a question. "Do you confess, brother, that you accept this sister as your wife and that you will not leave her until death you doth part?"

"I do," said Hannes.

"Do you confess, sister, that you accept this brother as your husband and that you will not leave him until death you doth part?"

"I do," said Elisabeth.

Then it was Katerina and Milo's turn.

At last the minister said, "The God of Abraham, the God of Isaac, and the God of Jacob be with you. Go forth in the name of the Lord and may God go with you. You are now man and wife."

The congregation sang a hymn, the minister said a benediction, and the wedding service was over. They walked down the aisle and out the front door. They were married!

At the doorway, Elisabeth stopped in surprise. What a sight! On either side of the walkway were pink and white flowers, dozens of gladioli standing upright in the ground. Where had they come from? Elisabeth had a mental picture of Grandma Katie's flower gardens. She began to giggle. Would Grandma Katie have done this? It would be just like Grandma Katie.

Elisabeth and Hannes began greeting people. She shook Hannes's mother's hand. His mother had been brought from Germany in time for the wedding by Mr. and Mrs. Burger as a special wedding gift. Now the Burgers followed her, their happy faces glowing. Then the greeting line moved on to others: Eleanor, who was in her class at Fog Hill, Noah and his sisters, and cousins and aunts and uncles aplenty. Seeing her cousin Virginia, looking lovely with her husband Anthony by her side, they hugged and greeted each other joyfully.

"How did you ever get the ministers to let you have all these flowers?" asked Virginia. "I just can't believe it. I heard one old lady say that someone was beating the devil around a stump. I just had to laugh."

"I think Grandma Katie did it," said Elisabeth.

Those flowers had been in Grandma Katie's garden. She was sure of it! Where was Grandma Katie? There! She was standing by the walk with Great-Grandma and Mama. Her wrinkled face looked youthful as a young girl's from joy.

"Grandma Katie, what have you done?" cried Elisabeth, hugging the three women.

"They are glads—do you get it? Glads! Rejoice and be glad! Gladioli flowers! A wedding is a time to celebrate. You see, I gave you to God a long time ago, when you were born. I prayed for a husband for you and now God has answered. So the flowers are my thank offering."

Elisabeth rejoiced. She was so glad her Grandma was a woman of an independent spirit. She shut her eyes and saw that long chain of women, coming out of the past, going into the future, each generation praying for the next. She was glad for Mrs. Weaver, her new mother-in-law, too. But, what of the men?

Then her mind turned to Hannes, visiting with the men on the other side of the walkway. Brave men such as Hannes joined the chain of women. Hannes who came alone to America. Hannes who asked God to let him marry her. Hannes who dared to keep asking Papa to marry her. Hannes who waited three years for her. Hannes the redemptioner.

Elisabeth whispered a prayer of thanks. *Thanks for Hannes who is a tease! Yes, thanks for Hannes who is a tease, for he brings me joy!*

23

The Windmill Still Turns

The scent of the moonflowers was rich and intoxicating. The white flowers lent an ethereal mood to the backdrop for the table where the wedding party sat. The wedding dinner was nearly over. Elisabeth looked over the lawn where the many guests sat in casual groups on borrowed chairs and benches. They were still eating, nibbling bites when they were already filled with food. In a short time, the rest of the meal would be gathered up and the guests would start home. Many of them would have barn work to do, late tonight. Elisabeth would not have to help with anything for one of the few times in her adult life.

Elisabeth took time out to observe Milo and Katerina. Milo looked completely relaxed and happy. She had noticed that Milo was often happy now, not somber and quiet as in the old days. And Katerina! When Milo began paying attention to her, she had blossomed like a flower. Her tongue had lost its sharp edge and her face was smiling more often than not.

The sun was beginning to redden the sky behind the windmill. *The windmill and Hannes and I go together tonight—gently turning and steady.* She tugged at Hannes's sleeve and whispered, "Look at the windmill, Hannes. It's our windmill."

Hannes stood and took her hand. Without comment, he led her from the yard and up the path to the windmill. There they were alone. She turned so she could see the people in the lawn. The first guests to leave were loading up their buggy. Hannes turned to her and said, "Here, I have something for you."

Hannes took a folded paper from his pocket, tucked the paper in her hand and grinned, a wide grin, from ear to ear. She opened it and saw that it was a piece of parchment paper, carefully written in Hannes's finest handwriting. She read:

*To Elisabeth on the day of our wedding.
Thank you for marrying me. I hereby
promise to fix the fire for the rest of my life,
so long as I am able, as a token of my love,
to remind me each day of my commitment
to you. I will keep you warm and make you
laugh. With love, Hannes.*

"Oh, Hannes," cried Elisabeth. "I love you, dearly. Thanks for teaching me to read and for your promise to fix the fire. But most of all, thank you for making me laugh!"

"I'll make you laugh! I'll make you laugh!" Hannes sang. He picked her up and spun her in a circle. Her skirts flared out and she laughed and laughed and laughed. Hannes spun her faster and faster. Then he began to sing and Elisabeth joined him.

Gott ist die Liebe, lasst mich erlosen;
Gott ist die Liebe, er liebt auch mich.
For God so loved us, He sent the Savior;
For God so loved us, And loves me too.
Love so unending! I'll sing Thy praises,
God loves His children, Loves even me.

Hannes put her down. Gasping for breath, she tried to hold herself upright, but she was so giddy, she fell over in the grass. She rolled down the slope from the windmill. As she turned over, she saw a blur of blonde hair, a wide grin, and blue eyes. She felt the hands of the man she loved rolling her over and over and she quit trying to stop rolling and abandoned herself to laughing. Her hairpins fell out and her hair came down and tumbled in rich waves of brown around her shoulders. When she came to a stop at last, Hannes helped her sit up.

They sat quietly, watching the guests go home, contented for a long time. And when it was dark and an owl hooted, they meandered down the hill, said their good-byes, and walked to their new house in the moonlight. The windmill cast itself against the moon. Elisabeth said softly, "As the wind blows hither and yon, so are the winds of the spirit."

Hannes added, "As the turning of the windmill, so are the days of our lives."

Sometimes up. Sometimes down. Turning, turning, turning.

Notes

This fictional, true-to-life story about Elisabeth and her family takes place about 1860 in the mountains west of Baltimore. Below is some background information and research that I used while developing the story and characters.

Women Make Their "Mark"

While researching my genealogy, I was dismayed to find that women among my ancestors signed their mark, an "X," not their signature, on deeds from 1850 to 1900. This probably means that they were unable to read and write English. Like many first and second generation Americans of various backgrounds, they spoke their mother tongue, German, in most ordinary conversation. Most of them also spoke and read German as the formal language in religious services of any kind.

Indentured Servants and Redemptioners

In *Elisabeth and the Windmill* there are two young men, one an indentured servant and the other a redemptioner. Milo Schrock arrives in America as an indentured servant. He has a contract, privately arranged, with Elisabeth's grandparents to work for them for five years in exchange for the payment of his ship's passage — a short time compared to other contracts.

Hannes Weaver comes to America before the beginning of the story as a redemptioner, not knowing who will buy his contract. His "master" Martin Burger had gone to Baltimore and bid on the payment of Hannes's passage, which was owed to the shipmaster. Burger bid the highest and in doing so, paid the ship's passage and whatever additional profit the ship's master received.

These fictional characters are based on the lives of my own ancestors. Some paid their own way to America. Some were indentured servants and some were redemptioners. And among these same people were those who became masters and indentured other people, especially relatives and those who were of the same faith or were from the same German village. One ancestor was said to have gone by horse to Baltimore to redeem a young man when he heard the young man was of the same church. His young daughter said, "Papa has gone to get me a husband." True to her prediction, the redemptioner married her when his contract was fulfilled and she was grown.

Indentures usually followed some basic conditions. The contract stated how long the person must work for the master, any amount from several years for close relatives to periods as long as twenty years. The contract also stated if the servant would receive a piece of land or tools when he or she was set free. William Penn included free land with Pennsylvania contracts.

One of the worst results of the practice of redemptioning was the breaking up of families in a similar way as that done by the auctioning of slaves. Brothers and sisters whose contracts were sold to different states of the colonies might be separated and never meet again. Children may have been bound out as early as eighteen months to three years of age. In these cases, they usually worked until grown.

Some examples of written contracts: she was to be taught "housewifery, sew, knit, and spin, to read in the Bible, and write a legible Hand." He was to be taught to be a "Farmer, read, write, cipher, 2 complete suits of apparel, one to be new." He was to "Read, write, cipher to rule of 3, spade, axe, grubbing hoe, and sickle, freedom." If both parties so chose, they could include a wage, clothing, a tract of land, teaching of weaving, shallop fishing, tobacco raising, carpentry, tanning, shoe making, and even terms of keeping the teachings of an apprenticeship secret.

Contracts could be sold or inherited. They were not usually recorded and not always even written. Some of the immigrants that were indentured were convicts.

One immigrant described how redemptioning worked. He wrote, "Every day Englishmen, Dutchmen, and High-German people come . . .

and go on board . . . and bargain with them how long they will serve for their passage money. . . . Many parents must sell and trade away their children and . . . when both parents have died, their children must stand for their own and their parent's passage . . . and must serve until they are twenty-one years old."

This immigrant also wrote that no one could leave the ship until his passage was paid, so the sick were the last to be chosen and paid for. Sometimes they had to remain on the ship for two or three weeks.

There are those who think that the practice of indenturing people was inhumane. Yet, how could poor immigrants reach America without this method of funding their travels?

The Trip to America

Conditions on the ship coming over were almost unbearable for many immigrants. Many times, they had to wait on board ship for the full cargo to be loaded, thereby compelled to spend their last money and use their food before the trip even began. Some conditions that plagued them were sea sickness, fever, dysentery, headache, heat, constipation, boils, scurvy, cancer, mouth-rot, breathing stench and fumes, vomiting, lice, thirst, frost, and storms.

One immigrant wrote, "These poor people often long for consolation and I often entertained and comforted them with singing, praying, and exhorting; and whenever it was possible and the winds and waves permitted it, I kept daily prayer meetings with them on deck. Besides, I baptized five children in distress, because we had no ordained minister on board. I also held divine service every Sunday by reading sermons to the people; and when the dead were sunk in the water, I commended them and our souls to the mercy of God."

When the immigrant arrived in Baltimore, the dangers of travel were not over. The National Road, going west from Baltimore over the older Braddock Road, had places of great danger such as the Shades of Death, where the road passed through a dense pine forest in which the trees shut out the daylight. In this forest, frequent stagecoach robberies took place.

Marriage

When the immigrants arrived in westernmost Pennsylvania and Maryland, they were isolated because of the sparse population in these mountains. Perhaps this is one reason the Mennonites and Lutherans tended to intermarry. My great-grandmother was Lutheran married to an Amish man, both of whom kept their own church affiliation throughout life. Great-grandfather was said to have faithfully taken his wife fifteen miles by buggy to her twice-a-year communion services. Although called Amish, he wore fashionable suits and a tie. There seems to have been much mixing of Amish and Mennonite people in marriages and social life in the community.

The Author

Esther Bender is the author of seven children's books and hundreds of short stories and articles published in various magazines and newspapers. She was a teacher for twenty-three years.

The themes of the books in *The Lemon Tree Series* rises out of her fascination with the stories from her family's past and subsequent research into both her family and community's history.